ALLWEAREIS
PUBLISHING

This book is a work of fiction. Names, characters, places, and incidents are products of the author's imagination or are used fictitiously. Any resemblance to actual events, locales, or persons, living or dead, is entirely coincidental.

Excerpts in the book have also appeared in *They Always Leave,* stories by Roof Alexander

Allweareis Publishing
Brooklyn, NY
www.allweareis.com

ISBN-13: 978-0615693965

TO BE HEARD

ROOF ALEXANDER

"If you are lucky enough to have lived in ~~Paris~~ Williamsburg Brooklyn as a young man, then wherever you go for the rest of your life, it stays with you, for ~~Paris~~ Williamsburg is a ~~moveable feast~~ portable second."

Ernest Hemingway

Chapter 1

ABE

I was being forced out of Manhattan. This was years ago. It was years ago when there were ten of us, sometimes eleven living in our illegal Chinatown apartment. In the building's half-century existence, it had started as a bar called the Black Horse Tavern, then it seamlessly transitioned into an infamous no-named brothel for several decades, and then came us, the ten or eleven kids paying as cheap of rent that one could find in Manhattan. No one came for the bar anymore, but we got a daily visit from a variety of old horny Chinese men. In fact, they came by so frequently in the beginning that we had to disconnect our door buzzer. They were unaware that the hooker's rooms were now occupied by what they call 'gweilo' which is sort of a Chinese insult for white people. Anyway, Manhattan was forcing me out, because I could only afford to live in old illegal brothels with ten other roommates, and those were tougher to find than you would think.

This was the end of 2005 and by 2006 our home would be cleared out for its next phase, the New York way. I decided that Christmas day would be the ideal time to find a new residence, based under the assumption that no one else in the oversaturated world of craigslist would be looking for an apartment that day. The $270 a week I was receiving for unemployment needed to possess a strategy. Being poor and strategy worked together like a couple of bad thieves.

There were two tabs open on my computer. One was for the section in craigslist called ROOMS / SHARED, and the other was an email to my mom. I hadn't been able to afford a phone in the past two months, so this was my passive alternative. The letter didn't say much because I didn't have much to say. Actually, I had a lot to say, but it was all about the numerous shitty situations that mom's just love to hear about. I spared her the depressing information by deleting the tab all together. Then there was first tab. It read:

NEWYORK>CRAIGSLIST>BROOKLYN>HOUSING>
ROOMS & SHARES

$500 MUST BE A HOBBIT! TODAY ONLY 12-25! –
(Williamsburg)

IF YOU DON'T MIND STRANGERS IN
YOUR COMMON SPACE. Bedroom private but small.
Must be small like a hobbit but not chubby like a hobbit.
This is ideal for a heavy sleeper. This is ideal for someone
kind. This ideal for someone that is either unusually social
or abnormally recluse. This is ideal for a writer. You can
smoke inside even though there is a balcony. You can have
a cat or a dog if it fits in your tiny room. You don't have to
have a sense of humor but it seems to help here and in life.
You don't have to be clean but most people will like you
more if you are. You don't have to be easy going but this
situation will drive you bonkers if you are not. You can
throw parties and have weirdoes sleep over with you if
they fit in your tiny room. Deposit: $500. Month to Month
Rent $500. Open house today only. Come by any time.
Push the buzzer. If I don't answer come back later. 99
South 6th Street. Williamsburg Brooklyn.

It was around noon when I started my walk across the Williamsburg Bridge. People always talk about how expensive it is to live in the city, but it's not bad at all if you walk everywhere and eat next to nothing and only drink from the inside of your pocket. It's the little things, as they say.

The day was bright, freezing, and empty. There wasn't even one other person on the bridge despite the brightness. The Domino Sugar factory stood as the lighthouse to my dark and foggy destination, the hope beyond the skyscrapers.

South 6th Street ran almost underneath the bridge. It was a desolate street with just a few rows of red brick tenement housing, the long awning of East River Bar, and a weathered yellow brick building with the words JOURNAL PRINTERS painted on the top floor. Every building appeared abandoned, but I learned later that façade was far from the truth. Occupied would be the opposite of abandoned, but there wasn't a word for this particular situation.

The 99 building was an old two-story wooden house that looked as if it could tip right over if one side wasn't attached to the brick building beside it. I rang the doorbell that I assumed didn't work despite what the ad said. No one answered. There was a large balcony on the second floor with the door open. I backed out into the street to get a better view. There appeared to be someone up in the room so I yelled, "Hello! Hello! I'm here to see the apartment!" A short man with a Mets baseball cap on sideways came out the door.

"Were you the one hitting the buzzer?"

"Yeah, it didn't seem to work."

"Are you here to look at the room?"

"Yes."

"It said in the ad, come back later if no one answers."

"Yes, it did."

He was talking on a cell phone, so I was unsure if some of the things coming out of his mouth were for me or for the ears through the air-wires.

"I'm sorry." I said. "Were you talking to me?"

"I said the ad said to come back later if no one answers."

"Is what we're doing now considered answering." I pointed back and forth to him and me, just in case he couldn't understand what we were talking about. I know I didn't.

He said something on the phone in the tone of someone closing a billion dollar deal. Then he took it away from his head. "Alright, I'll go for that. I'll be right down." That's when Abe opened the door to 99 South 6th Street and changed my life forever. I walked up the first two steps to the tiny foyer. There was a corkboard with fliers all over it, and about ten open mail slots with mail in only one slot. Abe ran all the way up the interior staircase. I followed behind slowly. There was a hanging blanket that I assumed was there to keep the cold out. On the left was a large open room with nothing in it. Up the stairs were three doors, the first one shut, the third one was a bathroom, and the one in the middle led to the room where Abe was hiding out. It seemed to be a mix between an office, a living room, and a bike repair shop.

Abe turned around in his over-sized swivel office chair and went into what seemed to be a used car salesman pitch. "Okay. So say you want to talk to your friend in Germany. What are your options?"

"Are you talking to me?" He wasn't on the phone.

"Say you want to talk to your friend in Germany. What are your options? You can use the regular home-line and pay up to a few dollars a minute. You can use your mobile and pay possibly more. You can use that Internet service... Voyage or something like that, and pay as little as twenty-five cents a minute, or..." He swiveled back around toward his computer, typed in something, and said, "Or you can sign up now for free, with Talk Cocaine, an online service that you can call internationally for just a few cents a minute, and all you have to do is get ten friends to join-"

I cut him off as soon as I could. "Wait, wait, is this room for rent just a scam to get people to join a phone service?"

"No." He seemed offended. "The room is right over there. I'm just throwing around ideas, ideas to help the people."

"Is this some kind of show?" I looked around for cameras. It was not a show on TV, but it was definitely a show, it was always a show without any audio or video or script, just Abe the director improvising his life.

"Listen. Just a few cents a minute to talk to your friend in Germany."

"Look, I don't have a friend in Germany, and I don't even have a phone, and I'm not really in the position to call Europe right now or just about anywhere. And we should go over the first and most important issue here… Talk Cocaine? That's what you're going to name your online long distance company?"

"It's a working title. Why? What do you have?"

"Give me a minute to think about it, but I can tell you right now, not freaking Talk Cocaine, not Talk Heroin, not Talk Prostitution."

"I think I see what you're getting at." Then something happened. A smirk started to form on his face and for half a second I thought he was going to blurt out, 'Got you!' But he didn't. Abe wasn't messing around. He was never messing around.

"So…" I peeked my head out the doorway to the balcony. It seemed to be very unstable, a leaning wooden floor decorated with random bike parts and broken lawn furniture.

"You're here for the room right?"

"Yes." I laughed. "Are you sure this isn't a show?"

"Tell me what you think about this." I followed him through a small bedroom with just enough space around the bed to walk to a kitchen area. "That's your room back there if you end up being the lucky winner."

"What does it take to be the winner?"

"Tell me what you think about this?" He put his hands up to setup the scenario. There was another bedroom off to the right and then a closet and hallway to the left that led to the back exit. "Tear down this wall, have one big room, and put in a long bar. Foxcroft and whoever moves into the other room will run the bar. How does that sound so far?"

"Super. Who is Foxcroft?"

"Foxcroft lives in there." He pointed to the other bedroom.

"Oh right. And we would be the bartenders?"

"Everything, bartenders, porters, waiters, managers, doormen."

I felt like this was a test, so I played along. "Sounds great. Doesn't it take a lot of permits and stuff to open a bar in a residential space?"

"If that's the route you guys take."

"Oh."

"This house was a bar and music venue in the eighties, so I don't see you guys having problems. I mean I'm sure they didn't have any permits back then, so why should you guys."

He kept saying you guys and that had me worried. "Cool." I continued to play the game, if it was a game. "So tear this wall down?" I rubbed my chin hair.

"Yes, a long bar that leads to the balcony bar."

"Do you think the roof will stay intact if you tear the wall down?"

"You?" He pointed to himself.

"Sorry, I mean, if *we* tear the wall down." That wall seemed about the only thing keeping the ceiling from crashing down.

He pushed on the wall and confidently said, "Yes, of course."

"Cool."

"But here's the kicker. Are you ready for this?"

"The kicker?"

"The kicker." He repeated.

"Then yes, I'm ready. Give me the kicker."

"This is where you and Foxcroft really come in. The bar is going to be 24-hours."

"Oh, I guess I *wasn't* ready for that."

"You guys live here, so whenever the customer rings the doorbell, you go to the slide peeper and ask for the password."

"Peeper? Password?"

"And here's the real kicker."

"There's two kickers?"

"Dos kickers. Are you ready for this?"

"I have to be honest with you, I'm not sure if I'm ready. I thought I was ready for the first one, but I was delusional at the time."

"Your 24-hour bar is also going to be all-ages."

"Dos kickers."

"Now, get this, I know what you're thinking."

I was thinking, or actually wondering, how old Abe was. He had to be at least 30 years old, but he had a baby face and dressed like a skater kid.

"You're thinking this is an amazing idea. How can I get on board?" He said.

"It's definitely cutting edge, and that's what I'm all about." Now I was playing the game that I still wasn't sure was a game.

"Do you have employment?"

"No,but-"

"Perfect!" He said. I never would have thought my future landlord would be ecstatic about me not having a job. "But what?"

"But I'm collecting unemployment for now, and I write, I mean, not for money, but that would be a nice addition if possible."

Abe began to pace. "A writer? Now, I have to tell you, that is a perfect room for a writer."

"That's what you said in the ad."

"Is that right?"

"Yes it is."

"Wait! What kind of writer?"

"Fiction, novels, shorts, and such."

"Good, good. You have a trustworthy face. I just spilled all this top-secret information. You could have been a journalist."

"Nah, no journalism desires here."

"I don't mind them, mind you, journalists. I live a controversial lifestyle and they come in handy when they are fighting against evil, but when they're a part of the dark side then, well, then it's a whole other story." He stuck a ballpoint pen in his mouth and walked back toward my future bedroom. "Let's take a look at the rest of the house. Oh first! Do you ride a bike?"

"I would like to, but it was stolen last summer."

"Summer, the best time for thievery."

"I concur."

We looked at the bedroom again. It came with the bed that took up the whole space. I followed him out the back exit in which the other resident Foxcroft used to get in and out. It was through a *Lion, Witch, and the Wardrobe* type of closet that went down a dark staircase. At the bottom was a storage area and beyond that a backyard. Well, it was more of a junkyard for bike parts just like most of the house. Abe told me I could piece together any bike I wanted. I assumed at that moment that I had the room, even though no one should ever assume anything when it came to Abe. "The large area downstairs is used by the bike coalition Times Up on Wednesdays and Sundays. They can help you put together your new old ride."

As he showed me around the house I could see so much potential. I saw a magical space that went beyond the fantasy of a 24-hour underage bar. Of course this was all before I understood Abe and his fly-by-night ideas. Of course this was all a long time ago now, years after that year of 2006 when the uncertainty of blank pages gave the world of Williamsburg so much possibility.

CHAPTER 2

NEW YEARS EVE

THAT Christmas Day, before walking back to Chinatown, before walking out of 99 South 6th Street for the first of many times, I checked out the corkboard full of fliers. Most of them had to do with bicyclists' rights, but there was also one that was for a New Years Eve party. It was at a place called Death By Audio.

"You should go." A voice came from behind me. I turned to see a frail man that didn't seem to care whether I responded or not.

"I should leave?"

"No, you should go to the party."

"Okay, I might. Are you Foxcroft?"

"No, he lives upstairs. I'm Seth, I live downstairs."

"Hey, I'm Alex. I'm moving upstairs in a few days."

"Hope you like strangers."

"That seems to be the sentiment."

"Only because it's true."

"I live with ten people right now so I figure it won't be much different."

"Maybe. No one else could say until it happened."

Abe didn't tell me anyone else lived there, and I didn't see anywhere else that resembled a bedroom. "Where is your room?" I asked. He led me over to what appeared to be a refrigerator. When he opened it, there was a small windowless room behind the doors. "That could get confusing." I said.

"Maybe."

I started to go back to Manhattan, but before leaving I asked Seth why he told me I should go to the New Year's party.

"Because I saw the way you were looking at it. I like to imagine that if one can imagine going somewhere, then they should just do it. You were contemplating it with yourself, so I thought I would help you make the decision. It's what I do best."

It was true. I had already convicted myself to be different in the coming year. The past couple months I had hardly left my room. I was working on a novel while trying to not spend any money, so I only went out to smoke a cigarette on the roof, or to take 3am excursions to the grocery to buy ramen noodles. The move to Brooklyn represented a change in everything. My new challenge was to constantly ask myself, "What would I never do?" The answer in that case was, I would never go to a New Year's party by myself.

The last day of 2005 came and I had moved in the three boxes that made up all of my worldly possessions. There was always a small Chinese boy playing down by my doorway. I assumed he belonged to the family that owned the print shop next door. He had never acknowledged my presence till that day. He waved goodbye to me. I waved back, I waved back more sad than I thought was normal. On my final trip back to Brooklyn, I walked over the Williamsburg Bridge with the last of my stuff in a backpack and two plastic bags. I turned around and said goodbye to the city, goodbye to the yellow cabs, goodbye to Mars bar and Sophie's, goodbye to Chinatown and the Lower East Side, goodbye to all the friends that didn't really stick, and goodbye to my old self. Looking across the skyline it seemed like an aquarium, or a train set, or a model city that I could just burn down in my mind. I was sadder about the Chinese boy than the city.

Each time I went in or out of 99 I saw the flier for the party. I had no other real options for the night, and there was a lot of self-applied pressure to do something I would never do. A plan developed in my mind, which was go to the party right before midnight, wedge my way into a countdown toast with a group, and hope they just accept that I'm a part of them. Maybe I would be so lucky to have a random girl try to kiss me at midnight. There *have* been stranger things happen, as they say.

Turns out that I'm not *that* kind of lucky. I walked down to South 2nd Street with my pint of Wild Turkey 101. There were a dozen bodies outside an unmarked door. I went inside confidently, sticking to my plan, except I was about a half an hour early. I was getting anxious just sitting in my new little room. That's what New Year's does to people, makes them think they have to be doing something important. I suppose I could have just sat there in my room writing stories about being lonely and such, but at the very least on the first day of the year, I had to give my new motto a chance.

I walked around the room pretending to be looking for someone I knew. It seemed like everyone there was locked into these unbreakable circles of conversation. My mind made up scenarios of icebreakers. I could just ask someone if they have seen John, Paul, George, or Ringo, and then they would pretend to know who I was taking about, and then we would be lifelong friends. Of course it didn't exactly work that way. There were about a hundred of them, either rock-n-roll or geek-cool. I'm not sure where I fit, maybe rock-n-geek. There was a stage with a band breaking down their equipment and another band setting up. Watching a band would be perfect. I wouldn't have to engage any of these intimidating circles. In the back was an open-aired room where most people smoked in the same unbreakable circles. I went out to the sidewalk to have my smoke. It was easier that way. The Wild Turkey was going fast, because I was bored and because I needed to get drunk to talk to anyone. I finished off several cigarettes between visits to the party inside. I went to the bathroom after these cigarettes, anything to pass the time. It was possibly the longest half-hour of my life.

A rock-n-roll man in a Cuban Army cap got up on the stage and announced that there was one minute left in the year. As this was happening, I noticed a girl across the room. She had dark wild curly hair and a young face with a pointy nose. She seemed to be looking at me, but I was so insecure at the moment that this concept was unconceivable. She was beside a wall ladder waiting for a rock-n-roll to climb down. I kept glancing that way in hopes of a connection. Before she started up the ladder I swore she looked back at me again. Once she disappeared into the ceiling I decided to follow up on my new life motto and do something that 'I would never do.' I followed her up the ladder. As I was pulling my body up to the roof the party began to chant the countdown. By the time I was up on the black tar rooftop, 2006 had arrived and I watched the curly haired gal kissing a guy in the darkness. I started to walk to the opposite side to light a smoke by myself, but a French female accent carried over the thick cold air. "Now you!" The curly haired girl was looking at me again. "Now you. Come here. We can't start the New Year lonely. That was last year. Last year we were lonely."

I liked the way she said *we*. I slowly walked over to them with my head down. When I got close she pulled my head over to hers and softly kissed me on the cheek. Amazing, delusional thoughts sometimes come true. Then I realized that's what she did to the other guy standing there, but I just assumed that they were tonguing each other down. He was quiet and nervous like me.

"Happy New Year." They both told me and I told them thanks.

"Whiskey?" I offered them my bottle and they both took small slugs. "Why were you lonely last year?" I asked both of them, but really just her.

"I engulfed myself in work and school." She said. "Every so often I would go out by myself and find a girl to fuck and that would be it." After she offered this blunt information, my heart sank a little bit. Isn't it funny how you can just fall for someone right away when you're in a desperate situation? She had saved me and then she had crushed me with a polite warning of sexual preference.

"That doesn't sound so lonely." George Henri said.

"Maybe. I guess it made it me more lonely because it was girls. One night stands with girls are like that because there are usually more emotions. Guys can just fuck you and roll off and you both can move on. I would prefer it that way, but it's safer to be with girls for more than just the baby factor."

I couldn't believe the balls on this girl. I looked at George Henri to catch his reaction and he seemed very indifferent. He had a calm face, an ambiguous face, his emotions weren't available. He was effeminate, probably gay, but that was hard to tell in New York. Many men along the L-train seemed at least a little gay. Nicolette asked him, "And you? Why were you lonely last year?"

"It's the way I prefer it. 2006 will be exactly the same."

She smiled. "I adore you George Henri. I know we just met, but I adore you, and I hope you stay lonely this year."

"Thank you."

"George Henri, this is our new friend. What do you think his name is?"

George Henri looked over me. "Something simple and American. Maybe Biblical? John, Luke, Mark?"

"Alex, it's Alex." I said before he went through the whole New Testament.

"Alex." She said with satisfaction. "George Henri, why do you think Alex was lonely last year?"

"I don't know. All I know is that everyone is lonely, so maybe the question should be, why was Alex not lonely last year?"

"Well? Alex?"

"Because when lonely started feeling better than most other things then it transformed itself into not lonely." I said while pulling out my notebook to write that statement down. "But… this is the real answer. As long as I have this, then lonely doesn't exist."

"That is a contradiction no?" She said. "Did you get used to the loneliness or did the pen and paper keep you from being lonely?"

"Well Nicolette, I swear on my American biblical name that I will always contradict myself."

The party became easy after we met. We all went down together. We all went down to the party together. We all went up together. We all went up to the roof together. Then we stayed up there. The band called Buried by Strangers were overwhelmingly loud, something I would have loved an hour earlier. But I found people that were like me, young desperate people wanting to fit somewhere in the universe, young desperate people that moved from different parts of the world to be with others that needed to be heard.

George Henri came from New Orleans, a painter as far as we could tell from his paint-covered fingers and pants. He was half Creole and half Canadian, probably in his mid-twenties. He ended up at the party because an infamous Williamsburg painter, David Bastille invited him but never showed up. "He's a real dick." George Henri told me in envy. "But he's doing it. International showings, local prestige. He's doing it."

Nicolette was a poet, just moved from Oakland, raised in Paris, twenty years old, finished her B.A. in English-lit from Berkley in two and half years, and then freshly enrolled in the MFA program at Pratt. She told me that she buried herself into a heavy rotation of open-mics and poetry slam competitions in her free time. When I told her I hated open-mics, she explained that she had to do those awful open-mics, because it was what separated the uselessness of creating and the purpose of creating. "I know that we all do this because there is this moment of bliss." She said on top of that roof. She said it loud enough to be heard. One set ears that belonged to a young man named Castor Hazel was the one set of ears that needed to hear it. He was smoking with a rock-n-roll circle beside us. "It happens when we perform or present our art that can't be equated in any other form, that feeling of making people interested, emotional, and ultimately feel what you feel."

Castor broke from his circle and came over smoking a spliff. He coolly handed it to Nicolette and said, "I won't discount your theory at all but it's not the sole reason why we create these songs or poems or acts or whatever. There has to be a deeper reasoning than the need to be *liked*."

"I didn't say liked." She said with smoke rolling from her thin lips.

"I'll tell you what you said, but differently. Say for instance I saw this very attractive girl across the room. I make my way over to her, maybe hand her a drink, maybe a spliff, and I'm subconsciously thinking about what I want from her. I want her to be interested in me, I want her to have an emotional reaction toward me, and ultimately I want her to feel what I feel, which can be attraction or just sexual intenseness, but at the bottom of it lies the truth, which is that I just want you to like me." Castor was what you could call a man that women noticed, tall, dark hair, dark features, dark demeanor, and good looking with something to say. In short, he could say what he just said, and get away with it. At least to most girls he could get away with it, Nicolette not being one of those girls.

"That is a well thought out metaphor that I can't believe you just made up on the spot. As a matter of a fact I have to guess that it has gotten you laid quite a few times, which leads me to this. At what point does the desire of being liked fit into people's art that trick's you into thinking they like *your art* when all they want to do is fuck *your art*?"

"Goddamn I think you're right!" He clapped once. "All these years I've just been trying to fuck my audience, I don't give a damn if they like me or not."

"I think." I said. "I think that both positions could be right. What's most important when creating is validation, whether you want them to feel interested or sexual or emotional or just liked, what you want is that moment to be validated, to be heard, and the next day you can either call them or throw their number away."

"Well?" Castor said to Nicolette. "What's it going to be?"

"She likes pussy." George Henri said out of leftfield.

We were all there for the same reasons. Down the ladder chute the music blared on into the night. An abandoned warehouse turned into an underground music venue. The building was first erected in the late 1800's to produce mannequins. It was said to be the first North American factory to produce anatomically correct female mannequins. This went on through the industrial revolution. Then during the Great War it turned into a canon factory. When the Great Depression came, the building was empty all the way until World War 2 and then it stored tank tracks. After the war it became a storage building for the Domino Sugar plant. The plant lasted for fifty or so years and that space became abandoned until some local musicians took it over. We were all there for the same reasons. It took all that history to get us there at that moment when the first sunrise of 2006 came over the horizon. We were the bravest of our former teachers, ready to go anywhere but home. The sun as our witness, we would be valid. The sunrise as our awakening, we would be seen.

CHAPTER 3

DELBERT PEACH

WHEN I had come home to 99 that morning there were several people I didn't know roaming around the house. They must have been a part of the strangers that everyone talked about. I went into my room without saying anything to them. I was dizzy, and happy, and freezing. People sometimes call this tingling. It couldn't have been more than twenty degrees in my room and all I had was a bed sheet to cover up with. I crawled under it fully clothed and passed out.

I woke up early in the afternoon because it was too cold to be comfortable. I stiffly walked out of my room into the hallway that led to the bathroom. It was destroyed from the night before. Piss, toilet paper, and vomit spots decorated the bulk of the room. I held my breath, closed my eyes, took aim at the water, and got out as quick as possible. It was somehow even colder than my bedroom.

There were noises of dishes being put away coming from the kitchen area. I opened that door and walked into a wall of smoky warmth. The room had an actual wood-burning stove that I was sure had to be in conflict with some building code, but then again, that whole house was probably illegal in some way.

"Hello there." A tall smiling man said from the sink. "You must be Alex?"

"I am, and you must be Foxcroft?"

"Yes, pleasure."

"Yes, pleasure." I repeated because my brain wasn't exactly in top form at that moment.

"How was your move?"

"Move?" It already seemed like weeks ago. "Not bad. Three train rides and two walks across the bridge."

"That's how the lower east side immigrants did it. When the Williamsburg Bridge was completed around 1903, this became the most populated neighborhood in the country. The Polish and the Jewish put their possessions on their backs and walked them across the bridge, just like you."

"My neighborhood was all Chinese and blacks."

"What part did you live?"

"It's hard to say, lower east side I suppose, but not really. It was at Market and Madison, right under the Manhattan Bridge."

"Oh CHUMBLES, that is a weird area."

"What's CHUMBLES?"

"CHinatown-Under-Manhattan-Bridge-Lower-East-Side."

"Ah, that's funny, I lived there for two years and I never heard that."

"I have acronyms for just about everywhere in New York. I like to think of it as code for my fellow bikers. Before everyone had cell phones we used two-way radios for Critical Mass and other protests."

"That's the bike's taking over the streets?"

"Yeah, it's almost accepted now, but there was a time when the police and even other random drivers would run us off the road, so we would have spotters with the radios telling us which way to go. Since the police could find our radio channel frequency we would use our own names for pockets of neighborhoods. Say we were down in CHUMBLES and the police blocked off Allen street going north, so the spotter would radio in to take OLE to STAB, which is Orchard-Ludlow-Essex route to St. Marks-Avenue A & B route."

"That's pretty cool."

"Yes, I also think it's pretty cool."

I took off my jacket. "I can't believe how much warmer it is in here. My room is an ice box."

"Yeah, that room has no way of holding heat. The last boarder tried to leave the door open with the stove going in here, but the walls just let all the heat escape, so there was almost no point in using it unless you get up every half an hour to throw more logs on the fire. It's a good room for spring and autumn though."

"My last room was a hotbox. I only needed a sheet, so that's all I have for now."

"Yes, of course." He went down the back hallway and came back with a quilt. "Here take this. The guy who lived here before moved to Florida and left just about everything short of his underwear."

"The bed is really nice."

"He had many nice things, he just didn't have palm trees and beaches." He said with a smile.

Foxcroft was easy, positive, he said yes to start most of his statements, and he made you want to say yes to most of his questions. He was one of the leaders of the bicyclists' rights movement. People didn't even know it was a movement, but he did. While he sliced up some tomatoes and avocados for our lunch he told me all about his life on bikes. "At this moment bikes are the only sustainable transportation that we have. Automobiles kill inside and out. Bikes don't cause wars, they don't kill babies and animals, they give exercise and joy, they don't cause stress, traffic jams, they don't take up space, make the air polluted, but now here we are, in the land of the automobile. It's a fight now, but soon, soon, it will be just a fact that oil will be gone, and the lazy and greedy will be leftover proof unless we are proactive in our fight."

Mind you, he said this all in a calm rational confidence that preachers would kill to possess. I was waiting for the question right before it came. "So Alex? Do you have a bike?"

"Yes, I mean no, I mean it was stolen last summer. Abe told me I could build a bike from all the backyard parts."

"Yes, let's do it. Let's do it now."

"Now?" I asked with half a plate of food.

"Yes! Definitely after coffee." He had an old stovetop coffee pot. Everything about that kitchen area could take you back a hundred years. I later found out the house was 160 years old, once a prestigious dwelling amongst shanty shacks and tenements, and now a jalopy without wheels amongst the budding thoughts of glass-walled condos.

We had our coffee and headed out to the backyard. Foxcroft patiently taught me how to build a bike from scratch. It wasn't the most attractive machine on two wheels, but it was beautiful to me. Foxcroft told me, "You want a bike that looks like it might fall apart. That way no one will steal it." But it was sturdy, built with love.

Unfortunately I didn't have the proper clothes to ride in those winter months, so I would have to look forward to the spring. I took a walk to explore my new neighborhood. Down by the river there were mostly abandoned buildings that represented Brooklyn's industrial dominance over the past century, but now they were ghosts from the technological revolution. There were some plots on the riverbank being ripped up to build Manhattan view towers. Just like many neighborhoods in Brooklyn, this one had been labeled the newest 'up and coming' spot for chain drug stores and real estate lobbyist imposed greenways. There's nothing that eases the suspicious complacent mind more than buy-one-get-one-free bottles of shampoo and the promise of a wicker basket picnic.

I took a right up Metropolitan and a right on Wythe before running into the most influential person of my life. This person told me his name was Delbert Peach. After all was said and done, no one was really sure who he was, but we were all sure that he was as close to a saint as one could get in those days.

I could see him from two blocks away. I thought he was a heroin junky at first, because it seemed he was doing the fade-out-lean-over that junkies often do on the streets of New York. But it turns out he was just bent over and staring at something on the sidewalk. As humans are prone to do, I stopped to see what was so intriguing. The concrete held the spray painted words: LIVE THE LIFE YOU IMAGINED$. I had to assume the dollar sign punctuation was an attempt at irony.

My immediate verbal reaction to the graffiti philosophy was, "God, that's depressing."

Delbert looked up from the ground and straight to my eyes with a delighted expression. "I suppose… it depends mostly, on how big of an imagination one has?"

"I suppose so. It still sounds like one of those motivational posters that always depress me."

He thought about it for a moment. "The correlation... between a dazzling picture of nature, and the nature of humans that forget to be motivated. I created that a long time ago with campfires and whiskey." He wasn't old, but also not young. He definitely wasn't the creator of campfires with whiskey. Delbert looked back down at the sidewalk. "I was just supposing that everyone actually lives the life they imagined in perfect sync to what they are able to imagine." Then he looked up and around as if there were something swirling around him in the air. "I mean... the ideas are out there." I followed his eyes until they landed upon the Domino Sugar plant. It was grandiose as a castle, as spooky as an old mental hospital, and the landmark that let Manhattanites and riverboat captains know there was another world over the water. It once supplied the country with three-quarters of its sugar. It once supplied just about every Puerto Rican family in Williamsburg a life. Now it was just a symbol of where they were, and where they're not. "Like that." He said. "There are very few eyes that don't set down upon that building, but once the image gets to the eyes, what does one do with it?

He looked at me for an answer.

"I, I don't know what to do with it. To be honest with you I have strange thoughts, and when I see old buildings like that I can't help but see them on fire, and the same with tall buildings, I can't help but see them tipping over."

"That's what you do with it. What about others though? Does one think that it is an abandoned building, or does someone think of the possibilities that a waterfront mansion like that could have, or does one think of how to turn the structure into profit? How does it process in the mind, where does it go? Does someone actually use it in their imagination or does it just die at the eyes. I guess what makes it seem sad or depressing is that someone had to call attention to it on the empty sidewalk of South Williamsburg. We may be the only two people to ever read it."

I still to this day, years later, hope that we were the only two to ever read it.

I had been in my new home for less than 24 hours and had met four people that would become my life for the next year. Nicolette, George Henri, Castor Hazel, and Delbert Peach. It would have most likely been five people, because one of the finest humans I'd ever met happened to be my roommate Foxcroft, and I know now that he was also one of the finest humans that just about anyone in Williamsburg knew.

CHAPTER 4

FOXCROFT

I could hear metal clashing against metal in my half-dream. I could hear wheels spinning and instructional voices in my half-wake. There was someone in my bathroom, so I went to the backyard. Foxcroft had shown me a break in the fence to take a piss in emergencies. Apparently our bathroom got a lot of use on the weekends. When I got downstairs there were people all over the place. It was the Time's Up Bike Coalition that held workshops at 99 on Sundays. In the backyard there were several guys smoking cigarettes and teetering around with bike parts. I told them good morning and proceeded to piss through the fence. Steam came rising up. It wasn't below freezing, but it sure as hell woke me up. I went into the large space downstairs. There were bicycles everywhere, upside down, on braces, on balancers, and in pieces all over the floor.

"Alex!" Foxcroft saw me struggling to comprehend. "Glad you came. Hold this."

I went over to hold a back wheel steady while he bolted it in.

"This is the stuff Alex. Look at all these degenerates finally doing something good in their lives." A couple of the bearded men laughed at Foxcroft. Bicycles and beards seemed to go hand in hand. The 21st century survivalist. They provided a complimentary spread of bagels, jam, cream cheese, coffee, and orange juice. Continental breakfast for the degenerates. Foxcroft saw me eyeing the goods, and told me to dig in. My nutrition level was probably at an all time low, so I didn't try to be modest. I went over and devoured a bagel. Foxcroft looked over at me with a smile and a thumbs-up. He was working on being the nicest person I'd ever met. It made me feel guilty for not being nicer, the effortlessness that is. No one should ever have to try to be nice. It should be one of our natural instincts. Somehow with all the thousands of lessons, words, numbers, ideals, and manipulations they forgot to install that first and foremost in our baby brains. But at least we all know how to add, subtract, spell, eat, kill, and jump. The necessities if you will.

I tell you all this for a reason. The reason being that I remember eating that bagel and that image of Foxcroft smiling and giving me thumbs-up and me thinking 'why can't everyone be as easy as my new roommate.' The reason being because Foxcroft was killed the next week despite all of the wonderful acts he provided to his community. While riding his bike, he was accidentally run down by a minivan. As he rounded the corner of Morton and Bedford the van came around behind him and knocked him right into a parked car. It might not have been such an enormous conflict if the van didn't keep going, it might not have been such an enormous tragedy if the man wasn't on his cell phone, it might not have been such an enormous reaction if he didn't kill the leader of bicyclist's rights, and it might not have been such an enormous backlash if there wasn't already a budding war between the bicycle community and the Hasidic community.

"This is the stuff revolutions are made of." I remember Foxcroft saying to me. "This is the stuff Alex, this is the stuff."

Abe was the chief mediator between the Hasid's and hipsters, born on the fence with a megaphone mentality. "This is going to be bad." He told me. "Before it was at least civil arguments within publications, but now, now there is going to be fire and politics."

"Which side are you on?" I asked him, because there was a lot of conspiracy talk going around. The Hasidic Jewish community had been trying to ban bicycle routes through their streets for years without success. Taking out Foxcroft was like taking out the General in a war.

"I'm on the right side. The one that is for the better good."

Foxcroft's death caused a big uproar around the city. Abe organized a special Critical Mass bike ride in honor of Foxcroft. I rode over to the meeting spot in Union Square. There was an unusual amount of cyclists out for that cold time of the year. Then when I got to Union Square, I couldn't believe the amount of riders that showed up. There must have been over a thousand supporters on their bicycles. Broadway and 17th Street were already flooded over. Police were just arriving to try and corral the beginning of the madness. Abe with the help of a megaphone began chanting "Foxcroft" and then led the charge through the streets. Cars and pedestrians were at a standstill. We went up Park Avenue to Times Square and then back down 5th Avenue to Washington Square. The police were able to get up front to escort the rally. They knew from the beginning there was no way to stop it. After Washington Square we made our way to Brooklyn. We took over Delancey Street and then the automobile side of the Williamsburg Bridge. Then the thousands of riders got to Bedford and Morton where Foxcroft took his last breath. The streets all around were gridlocked. Many of the automobiles began honking the horns. Abe on the megaphone started the chant, "Our streets." Everyone joined in until the honking ceased.

It took a special situation to make me cry, and at that moment the tears came pouring out. It was partially for Foxcroft and mostly for this large group of humans coming together with a purpose of defiance. Abe said he was for the better good, and this was nothing but the better good. At that moment, I knew if there was anything magical left in this world, then this was it. I looked around almost in embarrassment of my tears and saw that everyone was the same. Sometimes the right person has to die in order for the greater cause to live on. Sometimes that's just how life works. These people cared, cared about what Foxcroft represented, because he represented the best version of what they were. This was an important moment in our short history. Brooklyn came to a halt as we chanted, as we cried. The police sirens wailed as we chanted, as we cried. We would be heard above all these obstacles that represented the opposite of the better good. Our revolution had a heart. It had an identity. We existed. We existed together and whatever tag they wanted to put on us would be just fine, because no matter the title it was still us. It was still we.

CHAPTER 5

CONSTELLATIONS

SOON after the dust settled in Williamsburg, a woman came by to gather Foxcroft's few possessions. She had blue eyes and curly blonde hair like Foxcroft. She probably had a smile like Foxcroft, but she wasn't smiling. Her name was Arien, Foxcroft's sister. I remembered seeing her at the Critical Mass ride and thinking that she was one of the most beautiful girls I'd ever seen.

I went in the bedroom to see if I could help. She was staring at the wall where her brother had tacked up dozens of postcards that he had collected while biking across the country. "They're in chronological order." I told her. "He told me that these are what we have left, these pieces of paper with words and pictures showing that we existed. That really stuck with me, you know?"

Arien turned around with hazy eyes, red swollen eyes, and then she collapsed softly to the floor. I got down and held her head up. She was okay, breathing, no apparent injuries. An emotional crash I suppose. Her eyes opened to look through me. My fingers were tangled in her curly hair and when she tried to lift her head up, my hand went with it. She smiled at this, just like Foxcroft would have. Arien had drying tears on her cheeks.

"I saw you at the bike ride for your brother. I remember thinking how beautifully you rode your bike, and when you were chanting, the sun shone down on you and I swear there was this glow surrounding you, and I lost my breath for just a second." She was silent. "I don't know why I just told you that. Sorry, it just came out."

Then a strange act of life happened. Arien pulled me to her, pulled me to her lips, and we kissed, but not a sexual kiss, it was a sweet kiss. It reminded me of the first time I kissed my first girlfriend. It was sweet.

"Thank you." She said.

"For what?"

"For taking my mind away for just a second. I'll keep it with me forever."

"It's a portable second." I told her and she smiled in agreement.

After she had put all of her brother's stuff away, she looked back at me. I was waiting for some kind of sign to possibly see this girl again, but I was too blind to realize that the second was what we had. From the doorway she looked back at me painfully, and my heart thumped so loud I could hear it.

Foxcroft was gone, but his battle was just beginning. Foxcroft was gone, but our battle was just beginning. Foxcroft wasn't gone. Years later the people of Williamsburg would talk about him as a mythological figure. I was one of the new people. I was a part of the problem. The new people were part of the problem. Foxcroft had been there since he was a teenager. He knew every bodega clerk. He brought gifts to the Laundromat ladies. He didn't want any of this up-and-coming business. Just the new people wanted this, needed this. The new people would dissociate themselves with the people who had been there for decades. The battle was just beginning, and just like the now mythological Foxcroft, we would have to prove ourselves worthy.

A few days later Castor Hazel moved in. He'd been living in his band's practice space in Bushwick. He had a lot of guitars and towels. I showed him all the quirks of the house that started with the electric water heater. It ran water through a heated coil system, something I'd yet to see in my life. It was special, special in the way that it never worked. If the shower water was cold, I would have to go downstairs to reset the contraption. Most of the time I would get back to the shower and stand by ready to jump in as soon as the slightest change in water temperature. Then sometimes the special contraption would unset itself and I would have to go back downstairs wet and freezing to reset again. Most of these times there would be strangers hanging out and gawking at this awkward situation. If I was lucky enough to get the optimal amount of warm water, that meant that I got wet, turned off the water, soaped up, and then turned the water back on to rinse off. Long story short is that Castor and I didn't shower much.

I asked Abe if there was any way to get a normal hot water heater.

"Impossible. I just spent five thousand dollars on a telescope."

When Abe first mentioned the telescope, it seemed like just another one of his loony ideas. Most of his spontaneous creative thoughts either faded away as they came off his lips or took form in the way of a freshly lit sparkler. I shrugged it off as the former until the day I walked into his office. There was a box on the balcony that could have held a golf-cart or possibly a gorilla cage inside it. Turns out it was his super telescope.

"This thing is incredible. You can't just buy these in the store can you?" I asked him.

"I got a friend that's got a friend that was a janitor in a planetarium in Jersey."

"This was five thousand?"

"I like to look at it as an investment. One thousand viewers at five dollars a piece and the rest is all profit."

"I just meant that I thought it was more. For some reason I thought these things would be like a million dollars."

"It should be Alex, it should be."

Abe's current loony idea was to convince New Yorkers to pay five dollars to spend five minutes universe gazing. The Craigslist ad read: ARE YOU TIRED OF NOT BEING ABLE TO SEE THE STARS? ARE YOU LOOKING FOR SOMETHNG BIGGER THAN YOURSELF? 99 SOUTH 6TH STREET. $5 BEYOND OUR GALAXY TELESCOPE VIEWING.

Then my part came in. I almost always avoided his schemes, but this time I needed his offer. Abe was going to let me live rent-free as long as I helped on the late night shift. My duties included answering the door, taking the fiver, time the viewing, and letting the customer out. The funny part about this was that he could make more off my rent than the handful of people that would show up between the hours of midnight and sunrise, but it wasn't about my money, it was about the money that could potentially make the telescope a worthwhile investment. That made all the difference to Abe.

When the first late night customers came I stumbled downstairs to open the door. There were three of them, obviously drunk, looking for a late-night adventure.

"Five dollars each please."

"This better be worth it." The lead drunk said.

"Depends what you're looking for."

"Why? What's best?"

"What is the best thing to look for?"

"Yeah."

"I suppose you'll know when you find it."

The average customer sought out in me someone who may be an astronomy or astrology expert. I never was sure what the difference was. They wanted hard facts on nebulas and moons, they wanted mythical stories on constellations and shooting stars, but mostly they just wanted to know what to look for.

"What's the coolest thing you've ever seen?" A girl asked me after about a week of this nonsense.

"I once saw these two guys both dressed up as the Statue of Liberty get into a fist fight. I think they were fighting over prime tourist territory, but they were screaming in Spanish so I wasn't sure. That was pretty damn cool."

"You saw that through the telescope?"

"Oh no. I've never looked in the telescope. I saw that down in Battery Park."

"Why do you run something that you've never used?"

"I'm just here to take the money and let people in. I never claimed to be an expert. But I bet you could see all the way down to Battery Park. I mean if there were no obstructions. But you might as well just go to Battery Park. I suppose the whole point of the telescope is to go to places you could never get to."

About a month into the telescope adventures when I was really hitting a wall, the buzzer rang.

"Oh thank goodness." A lovely girl behind the door said. "There's only a few minutes left."

"Hmm?" I could tell I had very bad morning breath, so I tried not to open my mouth.

"May I use the telescope?"

"Um-hm."

"Did I wake you?"

"Mm-m."

When we got to the top of the stairs I pointed her the way through the office and I went the other way to brush my teeth.

"It's five dollars right?"

"Uh-huh." I pointed again.

She hurried through the office and to the balcony. After fixing my mouth and my hair I went out to join her.

She looked disappointed.

"What's wrong?"

"The only thing to see was a couple of guys sword fighting in their underwear."

"Does that mean something I've never heard of?"

"No, it means exactly what it sounds like. In that building across the street."

"I'm guessing that's not what you were looking for?"

"Not quite, but at least it was something."

"So what were you looking for?"

"Oh, it's nothing. It wasn't there."

"What?"

"I'm never sure how to describe it, but it doesn't matter. Maybe it was never there."

"What?" I pretended to be frustrated.

"A few years ago at this exact time of the Earth's rotation, except I was upstate on a mountain, it was right before dawn just like now, I saw this star alignment, but it wasn't just a few stars that I put together to form an image. This alignment made itself clear to me beyond all other objects in the sky. I thought at the time that it was how a real angel would present itself. It was the most beautiful thing I've ever experienced and I keep trying to get to it again, but so far nothing has worked. I heard about this telescope and thought that it might work. But, I guess that maybe there's a reason that we're not supposed to get back to those places in time. Maybe it would ruin what we had before..."

She kept talking and not that it wasn't interesting, but I was just completely exhausted. My body shut down.

She woke me and put a five-dollar bill on my leg. "Hey, sorry I bothered you."

"No bother. Sorry you didn't find your... thing."

"It's okay. I still have the false hope of capturing it again."

After she left I looked into the telescope and noticed a cluster of stars that seemed to be brighter than the rest. Abe had all sorts guides and charts about constellations, so I compared the coordinates with one of the charts. The star cluster was Aries. It was the first time I looked into that telescope and it made sense. I could see the appeal that Abe was shooting for.

Unfortunately not many other people would know that feeling. I got that month's rent for free, but the telescope scheme faded out and I was back on the $500 plan. The whole kicker of it all, and there was always a kicker, was that we never got a new hot water heater.

CHAPTER 6

CASTOR HAZEL

THERE are many places in New York that do not exist any longer. I was in one of those places finding spaces to write in my notebook. Chumley's was a hidden literary bar in the West Village. There were book covers framed high on the walls of every author that had been in the bar in the last century. I imagined my own book cover up on the wall. I wanted it in the corner of the back nook, just available to those eyes that preferred to search a little harder than most. The cover would be of an empty rowboat in the middle of pond with the title *The Arrogance of Uselessness* boldly across the bottom. I wrote the last words of my first completed novel. Wrote the words: The End. I looked around the old bar, taking in the atmosphere, trying to remember that moment forever.

The one beer I was sipping on for the past hour had gotten warm and flat. I wished I could have put down ten beers at that moment, but money was tight. I needed to find real work soon. My unemployment compensation was coming to the end of its promised six-month run. I went outside of Chumley's, smoked a cigarette while still trying to feel everything about the moment. I didn't know it, but it would be the last time I would ever go into the landmark bar. The building would crumble, the framed book covers would crumble, and my dream of being on the wall in the back nook would crumble.

I went back to Brooklyn, I went back to Williamsburg, and I went back to 99 where one day it would also crumble, where it would all be replaced by our favorite cookie-cutter distractions. Abe was in his office talking to a Rabbi. I said hello to the Rabbi, passed by Abe with a nod, and went out to the balcony. I looked into the telescope. Up Broadway was a man singing gospel songs into his generator-powered microphone and amp. He also played the electric guitar, and both badly mind you, but he still did it as if he had no choice. Maybe I could do that as a career? I needed to do something soon.

The Rabbi left 99 and he crossed the street in front of a truck. The driver laid on the horn and yelled something about a stupid fucking Jew. I had talked with the Rabbi several times. He was very smart and nice. He walked in the streets as much as the sidewalk, so the differences in the form of anger and horns were made clear. That was more common than not at the time.

I went to Abe for ideas. If there was one thing you could always count on with Abe, it was ideas. I had been trying to find whatever menial work there was around my neighborhood, but all of the artists had taken those opportunities. Abe was still working on his long distance phone call scheme. He had yet to follow up on his underage-all hours bar idea, so that ridiculous opportunity was gone. He mumbled out something about how he didn't have any jobs available, but before he was finished his statement he had a revelation. "Yes! Fliers! Street advertisement. I'll print out fliers for my long distance business and you can put them all over the city."

"That sounds good. I'm very capable of such a thing, arms and legs and fingers. Does it pay anything?"

"Pay?" He grabbed his calculator. "One thousand fliers, let's say twenty-five cents a flier, that would be two-hundred and fifty dollars. I'll take it off next month's rent."

"Deal!" I would have done anything. He probably could have said twenty dollars and I would have done it. The job sounded simple, but it turns out putting up a thousand fliers, or at least putting them up efficiently and spreading them out correctly was a large task. It took me four days at about six hours of walking each day. I didn't mind. It was one of those rare weeks in March that got a little warmer than normal, so roaming around the city was comfortable. I'm not sure how much business Abe got from it, but it ended up helping me in a round about way.

I walked into the Brooklyn Ale House on Berry and North 8th. It smelled like stale beer, wet cigarettes, and hot apple cider, all wonderful smells on a winter day. There was one lone afternoon bar fly occupying the farthest stool from the door.

"You mind if I put up a flier?" I asked the bartender.

"Go for it." She barely looked up at me. I looked her up and down. She was a voluptuous blonde covered in tattoos. "What's it for? A band?" She asked. You couldn't throw guitar pick in Williamsburg without hitting a musician in the eye.

"Oh no, it's… honestly, I don't know. My landlord has some international long distance phone call business, and I'm not sure how it works, but Abe claims it can save someone with a computer and phone a lot of money, whatever that means."

"Abe? Like Abe from the Times Up house?"

"Yep, that's where I live. He's taking some money off my rent if I hand out these fliers, a thousand of them."

"That dude is hilarious."

"To say the least."

"So wait a second." She thought about it. "Did you live with Foxcroft?"

"Yeah."

"What a shame."

"Yeah."

"You want a drink or something?" She said sympathetically.

"Yeah, but… no thanks." I didn't want to admit that I was broke. It's not the most attractive quality in a man, not even the struggling writer type of man.

"You said yes. What's your drink? Beer, whiskey, or wine?"

"I'm good thank you, truth is I can't really afford to drink out these days. But thanks anyway."

"Oh I meant it was on me. I'm not going to charge you. You were roommates with Foxcroft."

That's what Foxcroft did to people. I probably should have told her that I was his roommate for less than a month, but a beer sounded really great at that moment. "Okay, I'll take a beer, thank you."

I drank the beer slowly and Paige and I talked the whole time. She told me if I wanted some work I could be her late night bar back. "I need someone here with me when I eat, piss, and smoke. You wouldn't get any hourly pay, but I'll tip you out."

"That sounds great."

"Does cleaning shit covered bathrooms sound great? Because that's a part of the job."

"That sounds just like it sounds, but I'll still do it."

"Good, because by the time 4am rolls around I'm too shit-hammered to even count my money, much less clean bathrooms, so a part of your job might be to count my money also. Your job will basically be whatever I say at the time it comes out of my mouth." Paige said with a smile, but I could tell she was serious.

"I'd be honored."

She came around the bar and gave me a hug to seal the deal. I still had about fifty fliers left but put them off until another day. At that moment I was so happy to have found a job. When I got back to 99, Castor was playing a song on his acoustic guitar. I listened to a few songs from the bedroom as not to disturb his flow, but then I was too excited to wait any longer. I jumped in the kitchen and yelled, "I got a job!"

"More fliers?"

"I wish. Being forced to walk around New York City is the best job ever."

"Maybe you should be a mailman?"

"I won't discount that idea, Bukowski was a mailman. But for now my career is to watch a bar while the bartender goes to piss, and then I get to clean up that piss."

"That is a job. Let's celebrate!" Castor jumped up. "Let's get a pint of whiskey and go play on the L-train platform."

We did this once before. Castor played the guitar and harmonica, and I went around with a hat. We made sixteen dollars in two hours. Not horrible. This time there was a man with a banjo and foot tambourine already at the Bedford stop, so we walked over toward the Lorimer station. It was a much less lucrative spot, but our momentum was to be heard that day. Luckily on the way there we ran into Castor's band-mates, Lori and Connor. They were smoking outside of bar called Black Betty on Metropolitan and Havemeyer. I had met Lori once before. She was a bit deranged, but Castor said she was amazing on the synthesizer. Connor played the drums and he was secretly a millionaire. Maybe that's why the band was called The Secrets? Connor didn't want people to know, so he wouldn't lose his street cred. He dressed and lived like he was poor until it came to bar tabs. That's why I said "luckily" we ran into him. Now we wouldn't have to endure the lackluster Lorimer platform audience.

"Come inside guys." Lori told us. "Drinks are on Connor."

So we went in to all the five-dollar boilermakers and complimentary pretzels we could stand. Life at 5pm could be pretty great sometimes.

There was a middle-aged man at the bar with a ship captain's hat on. He kept up with us shot for shot. "You guys in a band?" The captain asked. It was an easy guess.

"Yes." I answered for them. "They are the world renowned Secrets. The Secrets." It was confusing, I think on purpose. "Would you like to donate to the sustainability of The Secrets?" I put my money hat out.

"Donate to the secrets? That sounds fishy." The captain said with a complimentary drunken slur. It came with the pretzels. "I will donate! But first we hear! We must hear your secret."

"Well if we give it away then it wouldn't be a secret any longer." Castor said, because he didn't want to play for this drunk.

"Just your musical secret Private! No others please. I'm going to drain the dinosaur. You can set up in the corner." He went to the bathroom and everyone stayed in form.

"You don't have to play." The bartender said. "He gets a bit over the top sometimes."

"Oh I wasn't." Castor said. "Unless you want to hear."

"I wouldn't mind it, but it's more up to the owner."

"Who is the owner?"

"The Captain." He thumbed toward the bathroom.

"That explains a lot." Connor said. "Fuck it. Let's play."

"I'll play for the Captain." Lori said. Everyone was all of a sudden amped to play. They needed a gig, and this could be their small start.

The Captain came back from the bathroom. "You know there was a band in the 60's called The Secrets. They weren't very great. Let's hope you're not the ghost of secrets-past." He laughed at his bad joke.

Connor took out his drumsticks and played various objects around the room. Lori played her blow-organ. Castor took out his guitar and harmonica, and they all sang the handful of songs they had written. The Captain was very impressed and offered them a gig. He needed someone to open for an act on Mondays called The Reverend. In those days in Williamsburg you took every possible chance to play even if it seemed weirdly religious. Sometimes life at 7pm could be really great.

After that we headed across the street to continue the celebration. We added The Secret's new gig to my new job and we all of a sudden had us a genuine start of a debacle. In those days there were only two bars in that immediate area, Black Betty and Spuyten Duyvil. It was an eclectic beer bar dressed in old school house tables and chalkboards. Their clientele consisted ultimately of middle-aged men with a severely above average lexicon of tech and beer words. There usually was one woman in the bunch that would have slept with most of the men if their need to argue about the difference between Swedish and California hops didn't get in the way.

We walked in and nine out of ten hats turned to see the newest experts or lost hipsters coming through the door. Only one hat didn't turn. That was one Delbert Peach, sidewalk philosopher and also apparently saintly beer connoisseur.

"Hello Delbert."

He looked up from his book and looked at me as if he had been waiting his whole life for me to walk into that bar. "Hello Alex. Sit, come sit. You have friends? Here." He got up from his stool. "Sit everyone. Delbert Peach. Pleased to meet you." Delbert had a large bottle in front of him along with a goblet half full of blood red liquid. Everyone introduced themselves, but no one sat down.

"What you having Delbert?" Castor asked.

"It's wonderful Belgium beer made from sour cherries. It reminds me of that sour candy War Heads. Do you remember those?" We all nodded unsurely, wanting to agree with everything Delbert suggested. He had that infectious quality. "I do love adult beverages that take me back to child-like nostalgia. I think it's only right." He told us all about the bar, the beers, and the people that I just explained. Delbert told us he came to Spuyten Duyvil every day. He told us about the one woman that was always around the bar waiting to get laid by men who could care less about such life pleasures. The woman changed here and there, but was always the same situation.

Connor was notorious for his anything-will-do standards when it came to sleeping with women. "So you're saying there is always a woman in here that is ready and no one takes advantage of?"

"Oh no. I almost always go home with them, but it's just because I like the idea of waking up in a strange place." Delbert said. That statement stuck with me, as did so many of the thoughts that left Delbert's mouth. The idea of waking up in a strange place.

Connor asked him if he minded if he tried to get in on the action and of course Delbert didn't care. Connor bought us all a variety of weird beers and made his way down the bar to his target. We all had something to celebrate; jobs, gigs, sex, and opening our eyes in strange places.

Castor and I drug our feet down the empty Metropolitan Street after the celebration faded into a causal yawn. Metropolitan and all its glory now, was just another empty street back then, just a junction for the BQE, just a shuttle bus freeway for the constantly broken L-train. No yellow cabs, no groups of tourists, no oyster bars, no clipboard causes, nothing but the street and two temporarily clearheaded young men carrying guitars and books. We took a left up Bedford and made our way quietly into the confines of South 6th Street. There was a Haitian man screaming outside our house. We had seen this act before, and it wasn't an easy situation. He was saying something in French, so we were unsure what he was angry at. We tried to sneak past him, but he came at us. Castor had the door unlocked and as we went into the threshold the man grabbed the door. I tried to pull it shut as he yelled in English, "Let me in!"

Castor pushed him back. The Haitian held on tightly to the door. "I belong here! Let me in!"

This was the problem with having such a loose open door policy throughout the day. The people that aren't made out of reason assume that they can come into the house at any time. We finally pried his fingers off the door and shut it in his face. He kept screaming and banging while we went upstairs. That's just how it was at the time, a mix of displaced cultures clashing. No one could claim to be from Williamsburg, except the original Dutch expats that were here when it was still spelled Willamsburgh. All others were orphans just as much as the hipsters. God knows, no one would ever admit that, but I'm looking at it now, and you would never know that back in 2006 this was still primarily a segregated Polish, Hasidic, and Puerto Rican neighborhood that was sprinkled with some white kids on the north side of Bedford. That's just how it was at the time, a mix of displaced cultures clashing on the brink of a major change. I didn't know it at the time, but one day soon this was also going crumble.

CHAPTER 7

GEORGE HENRI

NICOLETTE and George Henri became regular
fixtures at Brooklyn Ale House. Paige got used to me
doing just about everything. She was the personality and I
did the rest. That meant I did a lot of shots between
washing glasses. That meant I did a lot of shots between
cleaning the tables and toilets. That meant Nicolette and
George Henri did a lot of shots between their beers. They
closed it down with me one Saturday night. Afterward, we
took a stroll down Kent while smoking a joint. There was
something in the air that was so clear that it felt as if the
quietness of the morning screamed.

"Do you hear that?" I asked and they both nodded along. It felt as if there was something approaching like those alien spaceships in the movies. No actual spaceships landed. It may have been a freight ship. It may have been have been the booze, the pills, the weed, or the combination. It may have been just us.

We got to George Henri's loft at North 4th.

"Here's my place." George Henri said looking up at the old three story building. "I need to go paint now."

"Now? Now I need to go to sleep." Nicolette was loose.

"I don't really sleep. I sometimes pass out and wake up abruptly but rarely do I go to sleep." He walked into the building. The front door wasn't locked. Nicolette danced around a construction pylon.

"Come on retard." I said walking away. When I turned back to see if she was coming, I noticed the third floor lights came on. It was George Henri's apartment. "We should go up there and see what it is he actually does."

"We know he doesn't sleep. That's enough for me." Nicolette said. "Anyway, he would have invited us up if wanted us up there."

"I thought he did, I mean not with an invitation."

"No. He didn't." She said very mysteriously, and I wouldn't figure out till later what she meant. We went toward her place on Roebling. The sun was just about to come up.

"Maybe we should set him up with someone?" Nicolette said.

"With a guy?" I still wasn't sure, because he never mentioned a preference.

"Yes idiot, with a guy."

"He seems to be content on his own."

"That's the problem, he seems to be content with everything. He needs some drama in his life. Shake up that contentment."

"Sounds right for you, not everyone wants a good shaking."

Nicolette looked at me. "Just me huh? You going to be the one?"

We were talking nonstop right up until we got to her door, and then we got awkwardly silent. She waited. I waited. She lightly held my fingers. That was why George Henri didn't invite us up. He saw it before we did. I still think that we both didn't realize it until we stopped in front of her door.

"So I'll see you tomorrow?" I said.

"Maybe. When are you going to get a phone?"

"Don't worry I'll find you."

"Well, here I am."

"Yes, there you are." I went in for a kiss and all of a sudden out of the blue, just like a woman, she changed her mind. She turned her head, kissed my cheek, and said, "I adore you Alex. I'm not sure if I want that to change."

I remember thinking, 'goddamn women!' but acting calm. "So I'll find you tomorrow." And I could see her emotions change again. She wanted me to take her. Goddamn women. I walked away with my heart racing. She stood in her doorway. Goddamn women.

I thought about going back over to George Henri's to get his insight, but turned around halfway and went home instead. It was a good night overall and relationship talk or action would probably just ruin it.

Not too long after that, I was sleeping at 99 when the buzzer rang. It was a couple that wanted to use the telescope. Even though it was April and Abe had stopped advertising the megatronic telescope there was still word of mouth around the Burg. Every so often I would still have to wake up for this ludicrous idea. There were times when I would ignore the buzzer, but not this particular time. After they had got their fill of nebulas or constellations or whatever I was wide awake. I sat in bed for a while before deciding to take a walk.

This particular walk took me by George Henri's building. On the Kent Street side of the bricks was the dollar sign tagger. DEATH WILL FIND THIS$. It was hard to tell if this was pessimistic or just another form of irony. I saw that George Henri's third floor lights were on, battling against the sunrise. The front door was slightly ajar just like the first time I saw him go in, so I tugged at the handle and let my feet lead the way. When I got to the third floor there was only one door and it was wide open. I knocked lightly on the wall and walked in. I didn't see George Henri at first because I was distracted by the multitudes of paintings around the room. There were rows of canvases rolled up and stretched out everywhere. It was like a junkyard of lost art. Then I saw him in a trance, painting like a madman by the giant window facing east. The sun enlightened all the hovering dust in the room. It was all around, except the invisible bubble around George Henri, the painter painting without reason, distraction, motive, or sense of time. It was innocent, pure, it was romantic, a love for immortality.

I decided to not disturb him, even though it might have been impossible to get him out of the trance. He was blind and deaf, possessed by the muse. There must have been thousands of paintings laid out across George Henri's world. His style ranged from surrealism to impressionism to expressionism to realism to cubism to pop art to still life. It was as if Rembrandt, Picasso, and Pollack had a baby. I couldn't believe how many pieces there were. He had to be the most prolific painter under 25. There was a desk with a bottle of Old Overholt whiskey on it along with several different bottles of pills, a cereal bowl full of cigarette butts, and a small scatter of payroll checks. Beyond painting all of those potential masterpieces, George Henri paid his bills by contract painting, not something that he was proud of.

I couldn't believe that he had still yet to notice me. Then I saw why. He was passed out. Just as he said, paint brush in hand, mouth wide open, and leaning against the back of the chair and the windowsill. The rising sun shone over Brooklyn and on this artist. There was a glow around his head, a true angel artist. I shut his door upon leaving. Then after getting to the street I went back up to open his door as it was before.

CHAPTER 8

NICOLETTE CATHERINE-VITALIE

I began writing on the walls. I began writing on the walls when I couldn't find my notebook. I began writing on the walls when I couldn't find my notebook in my dreams. I rolled over half-awake, coming out of a nightmare. I couldn't remember any specifics about the nightmare, but I knew it was about fear. I didn't want to give into that, so I made myself a promise that needed to be written down before it was forgotten. There were several pens on the shelf above my bed, but no notebooks. I rolled over on my side and began writing on the chipped white paint. WE SHALL LIVE BRAVELY. WE SHALL DIE BRAVELY. NOT A COWARD AMONG US. I woke up later in the morning to these words in my face, noticing that I used the word WE and not I. This wasn't about me, it was about we.

Nicolette had a poetry reading that night. I hadn't seen her read live yet, but she had given me a chapbook of her poems. They were well written, long complex academic pieces might be the best way to describe them. I was hoping that she would have more passion, more rawness at the reading. I had never been hip to academic anything, much less poems.

It was still early, a couple of hours before Nicolette went on. Delbert Peach was sitting to my right, or I should say I was sitting to his left. He always sat at the second furthest bar seat from the door, leaving one stool for God knows who. Maybe me? While I went out back to have a smoke, Delbert read the chapbook. I asked what he thought.

"Close your eyes." He said as he put his head down and closed his own eyes. A few awkward seconds passed. "Now tell me about the room."

"What do you mean? Like name the objects in the room?"

"Whatever you think. Tell me about the room."

I had been in Spuyten Duyvil at least five times by then, always sitting on that end barstool, so I had a decent idea of what was around the room. I told Delbert that the floors intrigued me, the spacing of old timbers that could just fit a baby's foot. The beer geeks turned into babies after several of the strong ales kicked in, and they wobbled over the old timbers. The air was quiet and stagnant, and always smelled like yeast and old cheeses. There were these elementary school chair-desk combos everywhere, outdated maps and human organ charts on the walls, and a chalkboard that listed the beers by their origin country. There was a backyard lined with gravel and dirt. There were vines and metal patio tables.

That's when Delbert stopped me. "You see how the first half you described was sort of personal and very little to do with what was actually in here, and then you reverted toward just the things that you have just seen?"

"I don't know, I suppose."

"Well, that's what I sort of think about Nicolette's poems. She writes very well about the things she sees, but it's very transparent she doesn't actually know these things like vines and metal patio tables. She doesn't seem to know anything intimately. If I had to take a wild guess, I would assess that she... that she..."

"Hasn't stayed in one place very long?"

"Yes, she's like all of you, afraid to look back, connect to something that may give you permanence, because that could represent failure."

"Well, that may be true if you go paying attention." I said. "I like to think that I've held on to some people and experiences, sure, I put them in a story and mostly forget about them."

"Nicolette is most likely different only because she's younger, she's never had a chance to have an overwhelming feeling of connect to turn away."

Nicolette Catherine-Vitalie, twenty years old, born in Marseille in the South of France, her mom moved her to Paris when she was five, her new stepdad sent her to boarding school in England at age nine, when she was a budding teenager she was stowaway on a boat to Amsterdam, after the authorities found Nicolette her mom put her in school in Paris, a year later they moved to Miami with a new stepdad, she buried herself in self education beyond her normal private schooling, forging her parent's signatures she enrolled herself in the exceled program and graduated by the time she was sixteen years and five months, she received a scholarship to San Francisco University in their English program, and now here she was in New York getting her MFA in creative writing at Pratt.

I told Delbert this and he could see why her words lacked tears and joy.

"A poet lives and breathes poetry. Any one can write a poem. She is obviously a very smart gal."

I couldn't tell this to Nicolette. I needed to introduce her to Delbert. His voice was easy; it didn't come off as self-serving intellectual talk that seemed to be more common than not in the greater Williamsburg area. I invited Delbert to the reading. "No thank you. I'm meeting someone here later." He said in jest. I walked over to Pete's Candy Store, a bar over in the plains of the Lorimer Street area. The sandwich board outside of the bar read: HIPSTERS WELCOME. I thought it was an interesting attempt to be funny. The term hipster was being used all around Williamsburg even though no one associated himself or herself with the tag. If they used the word it was with sarcasm or irony, as if it were around them, but not a part of them. They wanted to be individuals within a large group of others that also wanted to individualistic. I suppose the cohesiveness of our subculture was that no one wanted to be a part of it, yet no one moved to a farm in the middle of Kansas either. Eventually the identity would make it to the middle of Kansas. The style and tastes of the sub-culture would become more about the consumerism than about young people wanting to attach themselves to intelligent obscurities.

We didn't know it, but 2006 was the beginning of unlimited information being ready available at our fingertips. Everyone knowing everything, which any philosopher worth their salt believes that once one knows everything, they know they know nothing.

We were at the beginning of knowing nothing, the end of knowing obscurities. At the time, we were hipsters, and we were welcome whether all the sandwich boards in the world were being ironic or not.

The rest of the board had the line-up of a few poets and a band called The Cangelosi Cards. Castor and George Henri were already there. We had turned into those immediate un-separable friends that came together out of a last desperate chance to believe in something.

All of this showed as soon as Nicolette approached the microphone. There were about thirty sets of ears there to hear the words in the air. She was drunk. Her poems were all new. Her poems were all about us. Her poems were about the things she knew beyond how many arms we had, beyond the smell of our feet, and beyond what any random person could easily discover about us. She told us:

"We all shared a feeling of hunger, empty bellies, bottomless appetites that when filled kept us up at night. When we spoke we shouted, all our voices together, a chorus of pleas and protests, rooftop dreams, voices carrying from building to building, no sky scrapers to block them, we all shared a voice, devouring the ears that accepted it, that opened to us. We would be heard. We would dizzily take in those sunrise nights and talk about what it would be like to be heard…"

George Henri and I were welling up while Castor stayed stoic. The other listeners there attached their attention to Nicolette until she said, "That's it." Everyone clapped loudly as she almost fell off the foot-high stage. At the time a twenty-year old girl still could drink in most bars in Brooklyn. Luckily she got out those last words before going into the drunken abyss.

We thought it was hilarious in the beginning. It was all in position in the beginning, the drinking, the drugs, the staying up all nights. The first night we all met we stayed up past the dawn and I guess it seemed normal to do that every time. We were bonding and creating and that's all that was important. If someone could sell that absolute reasoning and feeling they might make a dime or two.

The ragtime band came after Nicolette. There was a piano in the corner of the stage. The band gathered around it and took us back to what we have conceived as the 20's. There was a bluegrass and ragtime revival happening in Brooklyn. It was a time to get back to basics, people playing real musical instruments, people creating with pen and paper and paint and canvas. They were on the corner of Bedford and 7th, they were on the subway platforms below, and they were in corners of smoky bars just like that night. The Cangelosi Cards wailed out their horns and strings and voices while the Chuck Taylors tapped over the wooden floors, while couples swung their dance partners around, while another PBR can was clicked open, and while musical dreams blocked out any fears of the future complacent nightmares.

Then something strange happened that night. They came in with polo shirts, slick baseball caps, and brand new tattoo sleeves, trying to infuse the styles, yet so apparently phony that they radiated Manhattan Socials. They also wanted to be a part of something, they also would defy being a part of something, but the difference was that they weren't a part of us. They were a part of the ever-growing trust-fund kids latching on to the scene just in time to destroy its already questionable validation.

They seemed lost without acting like they were lost, like they took the L-train the wrong way, and instead of getting out in the Meatpacking district they landed on Lorimer territory. One of them started dancing like a hillbilly as if he was mocking the music and dancers. The banjo and washboard were a joke to them, unbeknownst where American music derived from. They went to the bar with twenty-dollar bills at attention. They wanted car-bomb shots, they wanted to play the jukebox, they wanted a bar with more girls, they threw the title "hipsters" out several times in a negative connotation. We were their Brooklyn petting zoo excursion.

All of this was chalked up as just slightly annoying until they tried to talk to Nicolette. Even the shit-housed version of Nicolette was smarter than all four of the Socials together.

"So what do you do?" One asked her. They were undistinguishable from one another, so I have no more description than that. Actually, the one guy who asked Nicolette what she did, had a diamond earing in his left ear. He was the one who stuck out.

"What do I do?" Nicolette played along. "I'm an optometrist." Thus was her answer when she didn't feel like telling people she was a budding poet.

"Oh shit. Thank fucking god. I thought you were going to say you were a poet or something fucking stupid like that."

"Yes, fucking thank fucking god that I didn't fucking get fucking cursed to be a fucking poet." She smiled at him, but not for the reasons he thought.

"I like your ink. That's a fucking sweet tat on your arm. I just had a whole back piece done. Took a total of thirty-two hours." He patted his back shoulder blade.

"Must be nice to have so much free time."

"What's yours mean? Mine is a tribute?"

"Mine... is a tribute also."

"To what?"

"You first." She said really girly.

"To like, success and having no fear. You know, life."

"Oh wow, that's what my tribute is also."

"But it's a bicycle wheel." He said still not knowing she was messing with him. And it was actually an old sewing machine wheel that she had done for her passed granny.

"You know bro, like the wheel of life, the wheel of success and no fear." She said in his voice.

We were all ease-dropping their conversation, staying close in case she took it took it too far. His friends were gathered around also. They were mostly complaining about the bar and people. One of the Socials was quiet, kind of kept his head down and held embarrassment in his expression. I could tell that I would like him without his friends. Diamond Earing hesitated before responding to Nicolette. "Get the fuck out of here. You busting my balls?"

"No, but I did lie about being a secretary. I'm actually a part of a dance troupe. We do interpretations of the sprouting of root vegetables."

"What the fuck are you talking about?"

"The dance troupe is mostly a night gig, so during the day I'm more or less a dilettante sonnetist."

"Dude. You're fucking crazy."

"No, what I am is a poet, or something fucking stupid like that. But of course those are just words that don't start or end with the word fuck or shit, so simple comprehension of the English language is beyond our realm of communication, so maybe we should just end this love affair right here and now. Huh? What do you say?"

"Fucking hipster cunt!"

That's when the shit hit the fan. Castor and I grabbed the guy's arms and basically carried him outside. Every person in the bar came for the other three. The one embarrassed guy held his hands up. "It's cool, we're leaving." But as they were leaving, one of the more verbally aggressive dudes pushed the banjo player. That set off a short brew-ha-ha that ended with the two main troublemakers face down in the street. The two rational Socials begged to take their friends away, and we obliged.

We went back in the bar. We went back in our bar with a sense of pride, because it was we. Around the beginning of the 20th century there was a group of artists in France called Les Fauves, which translates to 'The Wild Beasts.' They took on this name because their art truly began when their complacency was disturbed. They were done taking the roads that everyone else took, and as a group these beasts possibly started the greatest art movement in history. Those days of the early 21st century, insiders and outsiders liked to claim that the hipster movement possessed a lack of congruity. People thought we defied each other because that was the only counter culture that fit. This was not true in our parts. We fought for our identity and our culture. We fought for a purpose and our purpose. We would be heard beyond all those naysayers and skyscrapers blocking the moon.

I went home that night and knew that something had changed. Something small. A spark. Something small like writing on walls. I began writing on the walls when there was nothing left. I began writing on the walls when there was nothing left but to start from the beginning. The beginning of the we, of we the wild beasts.

CHAPTER 9

BLACK EYE

WE didn't hear from George Henri for days. I went by his loft, but the door was locked and closed. Something seemed off. I went to several of his neighbor's doors before getting an answer. The girl on the first floor told me that someone was beat up outside the building the few nights before. She said the cops came, but everyone had disappeared by the time they got there. She heard it was the guy on the third floor, but wasn't sure.

We tried calling him, but it went straight to voicemail. Finally after a few days of going by his place he opened the door. He had a swollen black eye and a healing scrape over his cheek. George Henri told us that he'd been jumped by two of those guys from the bar that night of the poetry reading.

They apparently were following us all until we split off and George Henri went home. He was really embarrassed by the whole incident and didn't want to talk about it or leave his loft or really do anything except drink alone and paint.

"George Henri. Castor is playing tonight." Nicolette told him. "You have to come. You are a part of us. It won't be us without you." She had a way with George Henri. I guess she had way with everyone.

"Also, Delbert Peach is going to be across from Black Betty." I said. "You guys have to meet."

"What about me?" Nicolette said angrily.

"Your time will come. This is George Henri's time."

We all would get our time with Delbert. It was inevitable that year.

George Henri put an army cap down low on his head to hide the black eye and we all went out. Luckily there was at least the three of us that would be there. Connor had about four sets of girlfriends show up and Lori Sue had some Burning Man posse getting weird in the corner booth. Black Betty could be filled with 30 people, and it did right after The Secrets were done. The Reverend was up next and he wasn't a secret at all. The bar got too crowded so we went out to the sidewalk, chain-smoked, drank whiskey out of a flask, and listened to the soul music permeating through the walls. After a few songs, George Henri said, "We have to go in there. Listen to that!" He was right. We did have to go back in there. Nicolette led us to the front of the stage, pushing past all the dormant bodies, and dancing through all the jerking bodies.

The Reverend was sweating and breathing heavily in between his musical sermon. The horns blew violently. The funk kept the elbows popping tightly. The drums crashed over the small room. Smoke lingered across the ceiling. The gospel singers clapped their hands high in between the praises of being alive.

We were all alive and feeling the omnipresent Holy Spirit. By the time the band had finished we were covered in sweat and love and toe-tapping harmony. Everything was happening here in Black Betty, in Williamsburg, in Brooklyn. They told us we couldn't dance, but we danced anyway, they told us we didn't belong to anything, but there wasn't a more tight knit group south of Harlem, they told us we had nothing to fight for, but we fought for the sake of fighting, fought for the blood we held in our hands.

Afterwards I took George Henri across the street to Spuyten Duyvil. Delbert was there in his usual spot with a woman to his left in my usual spot. She wasn't sitting in my stool, but kind of leaning backwards against the bar with one arm in a puddle of beer and her other arm propped on Delbert's shoulder. He saw me coming down the narrow passage way. I gestured to see if he wanted me to leave him alone with the woman and he waved his hand for us to come over.

"Alex, I'm so glad you're here." He patted me on the shoulder as if he was about to pull off a joke. "This is Delilah. She is a writer also. She is a very successful children's book writer and self-help women's magazine writer. Remarkable woman."

Delilah was about two drinks away from vomiting on herself. I got the impression that Delbert was trying to get me laid.

"This is George Henri. Delbert Peach and this is apparently Delilah, a remarkable woman."

"Not bad." Delilah said as if someone asked her a question.

"George Henri?" Delbert said inquisitively. "You appear to be of Creole decent?"

I wanted them to talk without me around so I asked Delilah if she wanted to go have a cigarette.

"I don't smoke buddy-boy."

"We don't have to smoke. It's just an expression."

"Gotcha buddy-boy."

So we went out to the back patio and did some making out. She put my hand down her pants and all I could think about was material for children's books. Delilah came right there on my fingers within just a minute or two. I don't recall that ever happening to me before. Delbert must have known that she was in heat. There's not too much he didn't know.

When I got back I saw George Henri smiling from across the room. Delilah went to the bathroom to clean up.

"How was the smoke?"

"Easy. Not horrible. Her wine breath could use some cutting, but everything else was in working order."

"Did I mention she writes children's books?" Delbert sincerely asked.

"Yes, and in women's self-help magazines."

"Remarkable. Women and children first. What a great motto. We have to remember that they have needs beyond survival also. I think we sometimes forget that."

George Henri smiled again. Delbert's unabashed perception of the good in all could make anyone smile. After we had left I asked him what they had talked about. He said Delbert commented on what a beautiful black eye he had. "He said, one day it's going to be gone and you're going to miss it. You're going to look in the mirror, rub over your eye and remember the day that violence and life came together for just a few seconds, and at that time you'll think about how all you have is endless seconds of just life. The black eye is your portable second."

After he said that I remember Foxcroft's sister Arien saying something similar, or maybe I said something similar to Arien. It was in the air and spreading. I was so happy that George Henri got to meet Delbert at the perfect time. I was beginning to think that I was a part of some heavenly order, like I was the guide that brought the lost to the sage on the mountaintop. In this case, of course the mountaintop was a bar, and Delbert was probably more of a saint than a sage. Either way, it was nice to be surrounded by so much spirituality in that churchless neighborhood that was slowly and painfully becoming my neighborhood.

CHAPTER 10

Williamsburg

IT was a Saturday night in June. Paige wasn't working, so I wasn't working. The other bartenders liked to clean their own bathrooms. I had nodded off while writing and woke up just before midnight. It was quiet around 99, no strangers using my bathroom, no house parties down stairs, and no backyard bicycle powwows. I went out to the telescope or should I say the telescope seemed to draw me out to the balcony. I looked over the balcony at South 6th Street.

Seth just walked out of the front door, most likely to make one of his seven daily runs to the bodega. There were some guys smoking outside of East River Bar. A couple of cars passed slowly by.

To the left there was a Coors Light billboard over Broadway that displayed the Rocky Mountains. The river to the right, the mountains to the left, and one of the most unique neighborhood cultures in the country in front of me. I looked through the telescope over the Hasidic community. It seemed very quiet, peaceful, the rooftops, the air above rooftops. Across the street was a building that seemed as if only a handful of people lived there. Through a window on the third floor I saw a naked girl practicing modern dance. I watched her for a while, her movement, the nakedness of her energy. The telescope gave so many versions of life; I don't think I could live there without it. Observing from a glass lens to the where the Gods shine down to where the humans carry out their orders.

I smoked a bowl and went down to actually be a part of these humans. I headed south on Bedford, crossing over Broadway, the divider of the Latino and the Hasidic. Shabbos was just ending by the three stars in the sky. I'm not exactly sure what three stars are supposed to come out before the Hasid's could come out and play, but there they all were, the men in their long black bekishe coats, the women in their shpitzel hairpieces, the boys with payot curls, and the girls in little dresses that looked like they were made two centuries ago.

I learned about the Orthodox Jewish community through Abe and the times when the messengers approached me on Bedford asking, "Are you Jewish?"

Even though I'm not Jewish, I look more Jewish than not. So I would answer, "No I'm not, but can you tell me why you asked me?" And that would lead to further questions and answers, and they always obliged me in the nicest way. That's how I found out about the siren that pierced through Williamsburg at dusk every Friday. The siren was the signal to light the candles for Shabbos. That's how I found out about the three stars that end Shabbos. They told me that Shabbos is just a weekly tradition to spend undistracted time with family. I thought that was pretty neat, and it made me miss my family. One day I would rejoin them, but at the time the light of my Gods distracted me. There were orders out there bigger than my loyalty.

I learned many of the teachings of Hasidic Judaism, and one of the beliefs that I whole-heartedly agreed with and tried to practice in my own life was their belief in the omnipresent god or the immanent presence of the divine in everything. It was nice to understand them more. Walking through their neighborhood that night, it made me feel comfortable being among them. We were all practicing mysticism, trying to figure out the relationship between the mortal and the eternal. I constantly asked the question, "Why would we put ourselves in this position of struggling to create these things that may or may not ever be seen or heard, much less recognized? Why couldn't we just live to survive and then accept what comes after that?" There is never a real answer, except that we never had a choice. Maybe that's the way my neighbors in the south of Williamsburg explained it also.

I crossed over the intersection of Roebling and Broadway, where the Marcy Projects and the Hasidic tenements faced off. At the triangle median, there was a Dominican woman mad out of her mind. She was throwing bottles at passing cars and screaming obscenities at the top of her lungs. Ahead of me was a girl that seemed lost. Once she saw that she might have to deal with the crazy woman, she looked back toward me. Then she stopped and waited for me to catch up. "Do you know where the J-Train is?"

"Yeah just up ahead a few blocks."

"Thanks." She walked slowly in front of me. We both quietly passed by the woman throwing bottles. We almost made it by without being noticed, but the glaring lights from the lamp store must have given us away. She came running at us while screaming something about how we didn't belong in the neighborhood. I had my fist half-cocked, ready to knock her in the head.

She was small, but clearly on a drug that probably gave her super adrenaline strength. Right before she got to me, and right before I almost swung at her face, she stopped on a dime.

"Fucking bitch, fucking white fucking bitch!" She tried to get in the girl's face, but I stepped in between them.

"Come on," I told the girl. "Just stay on the other side of me." I walked in between the two women while showing my cocked fist to the lunatic. The whole time she cursed at us, telling us in several ways why we didn't belong in her territory. Maybe it was true at that moment. It was still dangerous on those blocks in those days. The hipsters had been mostly accepted on the North side, but were still greatly outnumbered and unwanted on the South side. The crazy lady finally backed off as we got toward the end of the block, but still screamed at us until I got the girl up to the subway steps. She thanked me and we said goodbye without any other words.

I walked down Havemeyer, and cut over on South 4th to the little park with the large statue of George Washington. I opened up my whiskey flask, and shared a moment with good old George. It reminded me of something Hemingway wrote while in Paris. He had just been talking with Gertrude Stein about his generation. She told him that they were 'lost' and that 'they were going to drink themselves to death.' Hemingway stopped at a statue outside of the famous artist's café La Closerie des Lilas. He wrote: "I stopped at the Lilas to keep the statue company and drank a cold beer before going home to the flat over the sawmill. I thought all generations were lost by something and always had been and always would be."

I suppose we were also lost and I suppose we also would drink ourselves to death.

Delbert told me once that generations are defined by what the 'nowhere's' do after the war. But we didn't have a war.

There was the war in Iraq, the war in Afghanistan, and whatever other country that could have held responsibility for the first ever attack on U.S. soil. But this generation started before all the towers fell, and unbeknownst to every American, those wars were a long way from ending. This was about finding the last scrap of mainstream and fighting against it. We gathered in Brooklyn, we gathered in San Francisco, we gathered in small enclaves between these coasts, we gathered in the places that held a freedom to create, we gathered in bar room support systems. We were individuals within a group that rejected the group mentality. We saw how humans gathering together made them stupid and dangerous, governments, corporations, and religions. Once we became a group we would move on and keep fighting until that became another marketed and despised culture. But that was 2006, right before indie rock would become pop rock, right before skinny jeans would decorate the Gap display windows, right before the kids would turn in their baseball caps for fedoras, and right before Williamsburg became a travel guide destination.

I suppose we were also a nowhere generation. Just as, once you know everything you know you know nothing, the same goes for, once you can be everywhere you know that you are nowhere.

I left George Washington. I went down Driggs Street until getting to Henry Miller's childhood home right before Metropolitan. I sat on his porch and once again shared a flask moment with another expat. I couldn't help but clearly see the relation almost a hundred years later, Montparnasse, the bourgeoisie and poor artists finding a way to evolve together. Then they moved, defying space and time, Williamsburg, Brooklyn. They came from all over the world to be a part of these streets, be a part of the stone's throw city inspiration, and be a part of something they couldn't get in the malls from whence they came.

CHAPTER 11

A STOLEN LIFE

I left Henry Miller and ended up walking by Spuyten Duyvil. I looked through the window. Delbert was in position. He intrigued me to no end. Delbert Peach. How could someone like this just exist at the end of a bar in Brooklyn, no past, seemingly no future, no links to anything except sour cherry beer and the occasional desperate woman?

I went over to my usual seat and got some dark beer from Austria. Delbert didn't have much to say that night, so I began rambling about an article I just read. It was about a writer named J.T. Leroy. He was supposed to be this teenage junkie prostitute that wrote about his experiences, but it turned out that it was actually a woman in her thirties. The woman Laura Albert had just given an interview that she had been falsifying this teenage author for the past ten or so years. She said that she could write things as J.T. that she could never get to as herself.

Delbert seemed uncomfortable for the first time since I had known him, but he still managed to get out a shot of wisdom. "It's funny how when a fiction writer gets accused of making things up off the page, as if they expect them to defy their own nature."

"Then there was that other guy." I said. "James Frey. He just got busted for faking his memoir. It's like no one can get away with anything interesting anymore."

"Maybe, maybe not." That was the least astute sentence I had ever heard Delbert say.

"Yeah maybe not. There's that one writer from the 80's or 90's that no one ever figured out who it was."

"Who?"

"I can't think of his name. He wrote that one book... damn, I can't think of it. It's a weird name like generation something... It's... I'll think of it as soon as I stop thinking about it."

"That is how it works." Delbert said with a wry smile.

"Everyone thought it was J.D. Salinger using a pseudonym. Some thought it was Don DeLillo, others thought it was Hunter S. Thompson. But no one ever came forward to claim to be the writer. It's strange because people like James Frey and Laura Albert would do anything to be heard, and then there's this writer who has this option to be as big as any literary icon yet turns it away."

"Modern American nature seems to lean towards being validated, even if means deceiving one's self into thinking they are someone they aren't."

"What about you? You don't seem to need to be validated?"

"Alex, you and these wooden floors are my validation. That's plenty enough for me." The way he said it made me think that he was hiding something. I was already suspicious of him before he said that.

I had asked him before about his past, and he told me that he was born somewhere around Cheyenne, Wyoming. A police officer found him in the back of a pick-up truck with no wheels. The officer took him home and he and his wife attempted to raise the baby. His father was drafted to go to Vietnam and eventually killed. His mother became a hopeless alcoholic until the point that she could barely take care of herself, much less the then four year old. She turned the baby into the authorities and told them her deceased husband had found little Delbert in a pick-up truck. Less than a year later Delbert was adopted by couple in California. The wife was briefly involved with the Charles Manson family when they lived with Dennis Wilson. She got out whenever Charles shot the drug dealer Crowe. The social workers found out about her brief involvement when the murder investigations began. They took little Delbert away again.

After that Delbert was seven years old and considered too old for most families to adopt. He went into the foster care program and was in and out of foster homes for the next six years. He lived all around Los Angeles County including Hollywood, Beverly Hills, Long Beach, Santa Monica, and even Compton. At age 13 he ran away from home when he overheard his drunken foster dad tell his wife that the only way to make it in this country as a poor American is to go where the money is. Of course Delbert didn't realize that the man was trying to convince his wife to go prostitute herself out to rich men. Delbert went straight to where he thought the money was. That turned out to be the Hollywood Roosevelt Hotel. As he approached the hotel lobby, several cameramen were taking pictures of man and two women trying to get to their car. Delbert accidentally got in between the mob of paparazzi and accidentally tripped up the cameramen, one falling on top of another. The man with the two women thought the boy was trying to help him out. "Thanks kid." Hugh Hefner told him. "Come on, we're about to get some ice cream." Delbert followed them into the limo, still thinking that he should go with the money.

Delbert said he remembers more than anything that Hugh asked him what his favorite ice cream was, and it stuck out because no one had ever asked him a question like that.

"Butter pecan." Delbert told him.

"Butter pecan? Jesus, have you had ice cream before?"

Hugh took Delbert to get 31 flavors of ice cream at Baskin Robbins and found out his story. He told Delbert that he couldn't legally take him in, but if he wanted to do some odd jobs at the Playboy Mansion, then he could at least afford to stay off the streets. Hugh set him up with a job and a cash-advance, and Delbert got a weekly room in a West Hollywood flophouse. The old man running the flophouse was a junk-head so he didn't care who stayed there as long as they had money.

Delbert worked at the Mansion for three years until his sixteenth birthday. Hugh gave him an 18-year old playmate for his birthday present. Delbert let them think that he lost his virginity to her, but truth was that he had already been with two other girls from the Mansion when he was fifteen. Delbert told me that sexual freedom was for real back then. He told me that those ridiculous porn movie scenarios came from real life situations. "The plumber sometimes fixed the sink, and sometimes he got laid. That was the times."

After Delbert turned 16, he bought a Datsun 280zx, and took off to see the world. He said he was heavy influenced by a line in a J.D. Salinger book that said, '…all we do our whole lives is go from one little piece of holy ground to the next.' And that's what he did.

He went up north and picked grapes on an Oregon vineyard. He went further north and picked apples on a British Columbia orchard. He went further north and worked on the Alaskan pipeline. He came back down south and worked on a ranch in Montana. He went further south to Colorado and worked on the conveyer line at the Coors Brewery. He went further south to Austin, Texas and worked in a honkytonk bar called The Broken Spoke where every country musician from Willie Nelson to George Strait played. Then he went even further south to Mexico. His car was stolen in the Yucatan, so he settled in Cancun and became a certified scuba diving instructor. From there he traveled all around the world to tropical tourist destinations. He eventually came out with his own brand of diving accessories and had been living off of that since the early 1990's. I asked him how he ended up in New York City, and he said that New York was just another piece of holy ground that he was able to jump on to.

And that about takes us to that bar in Williamsburg, Brooklyn in the spring of 2006. After Delbert left I decided to follow him. I needed to see where this mysterious man actually went after the bar. He went straight down Metropolitan until getting to Kent. He crossed over to the waterside and took a left. I knew for a fact that there wasn't a single place to live on that side of the road for... well, ever. That road took you to Navy Yards and then to Dumbo and it was all industrial buildings. I figured he was just taking a random walk. Then at around South 3rd Delbert disappeared. I was about three blocks behind him. When I got to the last place I saw him, there was a break in the chain-linked fence that kept intruders out of the Domino Sugar factory. I looked around for anywhere else that he might have gone, but that was the only option. That Delbert intrigued me to no end. I didn't go any further. I didn't want to see him living bundled up in rat-filled shack like a helpless man. I decided that I would like to imagine that he lived in a castle inside the factory. Delbert Peach, the King of Williamsburg.

CHAPTER 12

OPEN MIC

THE time between her waking abruptly and her quietly shutting my door seemed like forever. I pretended to be asleep the whole time while piecing together the night before. Sometimes I blacked out before reading my stories in public. Sometimes it's because of the booze. Sometimes it's because of the anxiety. That time it was a bit of both. Nicolette had talked me into doing an open-mic marathon with her. She knew of two in the city and one in Brooklyn.

The first was at the Bowery Poetry Room. We walked in sober and signed the sheet. We sat in the fold-up chairs and watched a lot of aspiring stand-up comedians while passing a flask of whiskey between us. The host called Nicolette up to the stage. She read her poem *Lonely Night Women #5 & 22*. The ten or so people who were all participants held their attention to her words. I couldn't hear her because of my own nervous thoughts of reading. I didn't even know she was done until I heard the ten people clapping. Then the host called my name. I became very hot all of a sudden. The pages of the book I had finished that winter shook in my hands. I planned on reading a full chapter from the book, but it sounded strange out loud and I stopped halfway through. "Um… and then it goes on and on in the same way." I said. "Thanks."

No one clapped except Nicolette. She stood up while clapping and wooing embarrassingly loud.

The next stop was at Under St Marks Theater. It was crowded in the small room. Nicolette read three poems and they clapped loudly for her. She had something beyond her words that made people want to praise her. I was getting nervous again. This time I was going to try to read a story about my neighborhood. Nicolette handed me the flask and I downed it. She could see I was anxious, so she put her hand over my shaking hand. The host called my name and I heard it, but I couldn't move. He called me again not knowing who I was. Nicolette shook my leg and stared at me without giving me away. I stood up and quickly shuffled through the bodies until getting outside. Nicolette came after me. I lit a cigarette and handed it to Nicolette as she came out. Then I lit my own and sat on the stoop of Fun City Tattoo.

"What was that about psycho?" She joked.

I took a couple drags to figure it out.

"I all of a sudden started thinking about what I was doing with my life, and… and it didn't fit. I kept thinking, what if I'm not a good writer. What if I'm just another human that is forcing himself into a talentless art because I can, because it seems cool, because I want to bigger than I might be, and just because I have the opportunity? I mean, what if I'm really not that good? All the passion in the world doesn't matter if you're not good at it. It just makes one, me in this case, a fool."

"You know you can't think that way. You just have to follow the passion until it's not there anymore, or until you're not there anymore."

"Easy for you to say. You're young, ridiculously educated and really talented. You and George Henri and Castor are all really talented, and beautiful people. It's nice to be a part of you guys, but what if none of us do anything with all this talent and passion?"

"Fall back on our beauty?" She lightened me up.

"Ha-ha. Maybe you and George Henri. Me and Castor can't be housewives."

"That sounds awful. I mean not for George Henri of course. I can picture him cleaning the toilets and then painting a masterpiece. I could never write a decent poem about cleaning toilets."

"Well either way, I just had that horrible vision of the future when I should have been in the moment. I see versions of that horror in other people all the time, and I just started thinking about that when that guy was calling my name, that I may not be good, and that all of us might be wasting our time. Horrible huh?"

"I have an idea." Nicolette grabbed my hand and dragged me down the street. There was a lady psychic behind a table on the sidewalk. "This will be the coin-flip. Heads you quit, or tails you follow your passion until you can no longer breathe."

"Alright. What do I do?" She pushed me into the chair.

"You get one question for madam. Make it a good one."

First I gave the psychic ten dollars. No money, no truth I suppose. She asked my first name and then asked me to cut some tarot cards. After some shuffling she laid the cards down and explained to me something about the past, present, and future. It was all pretty general except when she talked about my present. She said, "Your expressions are being dictated by the pen when the pen should be dictating your expressions." I suppose it could have applied to just about anyone, but I felt like it was definitely relevant to my life at that moment. When it got time to ask my one yes-or-no question I chose to go direct. Heads or tails. Stay in the game or go to the bench.

"Am I meant to follow the path that I am currently on?"

"According to your chosen cards and the spirits in between..." She paused for a couple seconds and it felt more like an hour. "You have no choice but to stay on your current path. There is nothing else you can do."

It was relieving and a little insulting also.
Apparently I couldn't do anything else. Nicolette seemed
happier than I did at that moment. She looked at me like
that one night outside her door. We took off into the streets
of Manhattan, caught the L into Brooklyn, and ran over to
Galapagos for the last open-mic. This time with a steady
flask in one hand and *The Kids Are Dancing Again* in the
other hand, I stepped up on stage and shouted through my
pen:

"I see the kids are dancing again?" He said as a
question, a question she knew after sixty or so years that
she didn't have to answer. "I didn't know if it was going to
happen, but sure as corn, sure as corn they're doing it."
He was all of a sudden in the mood for corn, but
unfortunately he couldn't eat corn any longer. Even his
fake teeth couldn't handle the little chewy bastards. "I
suppose it was the arms, all locked up, all folded and
locked up." He said. "Because it wasn't they're feet. You
saw them… moving this way and that." She turned her
head toward him to imply that he should stop being such a
nincompoop. They were on a no-words relationship. They
had their little sidewalk patio outside their apartment on
Berry and North 7th where they would sit for hours at a
time to people watch and chain smoke cigarettes.

A small, not to say petite bearded man came skipping down the middle of the North 7th Street. He was dressed as a fairy. He held a magic wand. He skipped past the corner while babbling on about granting wishes.

They said nothing about this.

A few minutes later, a lesbian couple passed by holding hands, laughing, and cursing like sailors. They were sporting trucker hats, overalls, and old-school b-ball sneakers.

They said nothing about this.

A short time later, two guys covered in tattoos rode by on skateboards, one was smoking and the other held a puppet parrot that he made squawking noises with.

They said nothing about this.

Then not too long after that an indistinct man came walking down their sidewalk simply with a banana in his hand. He passed without incident.

"There isn't too many things in this world you can trust." He told his wife. "But if there's one thing that comes to mind, it's a man walking down the street with a banana in his hand. Now that's an ease, that's something you can trust."

She once again forcibly turned her head to look at him for a long second as if he had mustard on his face.

"Maybe that's why the kids are dancing again? Maybe it's because they took the bananas out of their hands."

That corner on Berry and North 7th used to be just the wind. They took from the wind, and then passed it on. They took from the books, and passed it on. They took from music, and passed it on.

And everything used to be amazing, but now they just danced. And everything used to be for sure, but now they just danced. Dazzled by their own scruples, by their surety, by their baffled amazedness, they stood their ground, ready at any moment for the next song to begin.

After I was done, the attentive small crowd clapped loudly and my heart warmed up with a new comfort. Nicolette got us celebration shots.

And that's what I remember, not including the briefs moments of stumbling home, the brief moments of making out under the Williamsburg Bridge, and the brief moments of having sex in my little room at 99. Then all there was left was me alone in my bed and I had an overwhelming feeling it might be awhile before I saw Nicolette again.

CHAPTER 13

THE WIZARD OF WILLIAMSBURG

I didn't see Nicolette for a long time after that night. Other people saw her for a short period before her disappearance. George Henri told me that every time my name was brought up she would change the subject. Castor told me she would just walk away when he joked about our one-night stand.

I didn't let it bother me too much. I got back to focusing on the book, which is what we do when the girl is gone. I told her the first night we met that I would never be lonely as long as I had my pen and paper, and those days I was ready to prove everybody wrong as much as prove myself right.

In between the book and working at the Brooklyn Ale House and Abe's constant ideas blossoming around 99, I was able to take in some Delbert Peach time.

"Your friends have been coming by to see me." Delbert sat to my right as usual.

"Oh yeah?" This oddly surprised me in the way that I thought Delbert was my discovery and that my friends should only see him through my supervision. "Are they planning an intervention for me or something?"

"No, they all wanted some sort of life advice."

"I apologize for that. I just always tell them all the enlightening things you say, and they probably assumed you were here for the world." Once again I brought it back to me. It was almost like I was jealous.

"Oh it's fine. I suppose we're all here for the world in some way. My way is always being in the same spot in the universe, accessible to most means."

"I suppose so." I wanted to know why Nicolette came to him more than the others, so of course I asked him about everyone. "So what did they ask you?"

"It's funny, because all three of them essentially wanted life advice, but what they asked me was *art* advice."

By his tone I could tell there was something wrong with that concept. "Are you saying that they asked the wrong questions?"

"Well, the problem with this is, life advice can ruin one's art, and art advice can ruin one's life."

"What about Nicolette?" I stopped beating around the bush as they say.

"Nicolette. She needed her life ruined the most. You two must have had some relations."

"Yeah, did she say something about it?"

"No, I just could tell how she didn't mention your name once even when she said things about what would have been you. The first time I met her she said your name every other sentence even though you were standing right beside her, as if you were this higher entity."

"Really? I never noticed."

"Of course you didn't. Flattery seeps in comfortably."

"Then what did she say?" I kept pushing.

"She wanted permission to be self-destructive."

I laughed. "I think she's already got that covered."

"Not really. It seems her whole life she's been destructive to the things she doesn't really care about. She has preserved herself throughout, projecting this destructiveness seemingly on herself, but it all falls to others around her. I told her there is only one true form of the artist, and it is called the poet. This poet may or may not actually write poems on a piece of paper, that's optional. The true poet's poems are in the actions they take in life, the controlled drama they put into their minds, the brave changes they make to create discomfort. She said that's the kind of poet she wanted to be. I told her the first step would be the realization that universities don't make poets, no matter how many pieces of paper they give out."

"And?"

"And she got this determined look in her eyes and left without finishing her beer."

"Well shit." I said. "That doesn't sound good."

"Once again, it depends on what one is looking to ruin."

"What about Castor and George Henri? What are they looking to ruin?"

"George Henri, like all of us, was just concerned about direction and most of all his authenticity. I told him that the true painter must be willing to burn everything he has created and start over, otherwise you might as well be painting those yellow lines in the streets."

"You're like the Wizard of Oz. The Wizard of Williamsburg."

I never had heard Delbert laugh out loud. He almost cackled in embarrassment after I game him the title. "I'm going to need a bigger curtain for that status."

"What else Wiz? Did you give Castor a heart?"

"Actually the opposite. He had temporarily lost his punch. I told him rock musicians are just boxers with instruments instead of gloves. Just like boxers they get tired. I told him he could either both retire and become a trainer, or keep getting in the ring and punching. And most importantly, taking the punches thrown at you."

CHAPTER 14

PUNCHES

THE Secrets got a gig at a bar called Pianos in the Lower East Side. Ludlow Street was quickly becoming a joke, but it still had a handful of the best small music clubs in the city. If you could swim through the ocean of Upper East Side frat boys, the misplaced Wall Street suits, and the extraordinarily loud bridge and tunnel tribes, then you might be able to see a decent band. The Secrets were tucked in between a rock band from Philly called Robes and a pop duo from Boston called Anything but Animals.

The door host crossed my name off the list along with George Henri's. I saw Nicolette's name uncrossed. I was hoping that she could forget about our little sexual drama to support Castor for the night. There were two indie labels there to see The Secrets. The night they played Black Betty there was a writer from the L-Magazine in the small audience. The band landed in an issue of the magazine under the title *Williamsburg Bands You've Never Heard That You Have To Hear*.

The room was about three-quarters full, mostly white guys around 25 with beards and glasses that followed L-Magazine recommendations religiously. Right before Castor took the stage George Henri whispered to me, "Don't say anything right now, but those guys that jumped me are here."

"Here?" I started to look around while the band got set to play.

"Yes, in the front bar, not in here."

"What do you want to do?"

"Nothing, let's just watch the show and get out." George Henri said.

"Okay, okay." He was getting emotional. "Go to the front, to the stage. I'll meet you there in a second." I went to scout out the situation. Then I heard over the microphone. "Alex? We're about to start." Castor said in his serious sounding joking voice. "Where are you going buddy?"

I flipped him off and went to the front bar. I saw the two of them right away, recognizable by the one guy with the sleeve and diamond earing. I was trying to be sneaky, but I guess my hatred for them glowed because they turned around and looked right at me. It was hard to tell if they knew who I was, but either way I turned back around and went to the back room. The band had just started. The sound was incredible. No one including the band had ever heard their music over a loud clean sound system before. I was up front with George Henri. It was almost too loud. I looked around to gauge the audience's reaction after the song ended and they went nuts. Right as the band was going into the second song I saw the two troublemakers come into the back room. I kept one eye on them and one on the band.

The same reaction came after their second song ended, except along with the thunder of claps came some obnoxious boos. Castor's cool demeanor was thrown off. He put his hand above his eyes to block the spotlight shining down on him. Connor started up the next song on the drums and Castor put his hand back on his guitar. The Socials were trying to heckle the band, but the music was too loud to hear anything. Once again after the song ended the claps and boos joined together. Castor shot daggers across the room trying to figure out who the culprits were. Later on he told me that the whole night he kept repeating in his head what Delbert told him. "Keep throwing punches. Fight, fight, fight!"

As soon as he found and recognized the two hecklers, he dropped his guitar and jumped into the audience with the cordless microphone in hand. I followed close behind him, mostly just trying to stop him, but he was more determined than me. By the time I got to them Castor was beating the diamond earing guy with the microphone. You could hear the thumping over the sound system. I took down the other guy. We exchanged a few punches that didn't do much damage. By the time security had separated us all, the diamond earing guy's face was covered in blood. Castor held the bloody microphone high in the air as he got drug out of the club.

The police came and arrested Castor. An ambulance also came to take away the diamond earing guy. George Henri was so happy that he cried. He told me that no one had ever taken up for him in his whole life. Diamond earing's injuries looked worse than they were. He never pressed charges because he knew that George Henri would also press charges against him and his friend. Connor bailed out Castor the next day with good and bad news. The bad news was that the two representatives from the indie labels decided to pass. "They said they couldn't represent acts that were unstable." Connor told him.

Castor was livid. "If this were the 70's the music labels would be lining up to sign us. Ozzie bit the head off a goddamn dove for Christ sake. All I did was beat up a heckler!"

"With a microphone." I added in, and he couldn't help but break a smile.

"That's true. It was a loud deadly weapon."

The good news was that a lot of those guys with beards and glasses at the show were music bloggers. The Internet rang the praises of The Secrets. 'Three rocking songs and one rocking fight!' The Secrets were more popular than ever after playing 1.3 shows.

CHAPTER 15

BURN EVERYTHING

THE summer had rapidly come upon us at 99. The upstairs area was an inferno. Abe bought six fans and strategically placed them to create a whirlwind, but unless you were right in the path of the tornado it was still a sweaty mess. The only salvation of the heat was that the cold showers finally worked to our advantage. But as every upside in 99, there was a downside. There was refreshing cold water, but at the time you had to battle through an army of blackflies that had taken over the bathroom. There was never a dull moment for $500 a month.

Nicolette had completely disappeared. Her phone went straight to voicemail. I saw one of her classmates and he said that she had dropped out of school. George Henri went by her apartment and her neighbor told him that she moved out.

We assumed that she moved away from the city until I saw one of her former girl hook-ups at Brooklyn Ale House. She said that Nicolette had been around the Metropolitan on Wednesdays, which was lesbian night. George Henri wanted to go find her there, but I couldn't go after someone that was avoiding me. He agreed, but was sad about it, probably sadder than me. Our gang wasn't the same without her.

I would go out to my balcony at night and look across Williamsburg hoping to see her. She had the uncanny ability of staying out of my sight, even through the telescope. Down below the crazy Haitian would be screaming something only he understood. As the weather got warmer, he was out there nightly and becoming more of a nuisance. I asked Abe about him, about what we should do. He told me, "You know these situations have always been here. In the past you defend your block if it's too much. In the past if you live in a defined area and there's a problem, you take care of the problem. Now, people call 311, or they call the police, people put their head down and walk by fast. There's nothing wrong with defending your territory if it's just."

"Does he not bother you?"

"That guy? I suppose he does." Abe said. "But I can't let anything bother me in this neighborhood to the point where I react beyond my means. I'm like a politician. I have to stay neutral in many situations to help the greater good."

It was true. He was the great South Side mediator. Bringing together the Hasid's, the Hipsters, and the Latinos. He was the only person I had ever met that spoke Yiddish, Spanish, and Hipsterish. I started to leave, but then I heard Abe yell, "Chickens!"

"I'm sorry? What's that?"

"Chickens!"

"Who?"

"No, not who, when."

"Okay. When?"

"Tomorrow. We'll start tomorrow."

"Fantastic."

I had seen this before. He has a ridiculous plan that no one's going to talk him out of. "What do we need to do first?"

"Chickens. First we get the chickens."

"Is this a new gang in the hood? A Haitian gang?" I was half-joking.

"No, they're chickens. I'm having them shipped here tomorrow. We're starting a chicken farm. Fresh eggs everyday. And no more beetles!"

"Beetles?"

I woke up the next afternoon to the squawking of chickens. They were a little louder than the noise of the six fans. I went out to the backyard. In a little less than 24 hours Abe had managed to turn the bicycle scrapyard into a mini chicken farm. There were four chickens pecking at the nuts and bolts that littered the backyard.

"Who are your new friends?" I asked Abe, who by the way, couldn't be prouder of his farm.

"The red one is Lucy, the brown one is Mohammad, the white one is Gene Wilder, and the black one is Sammy Davis Jr."

"Shouldn't the black chicken be Richard Pryor?"

"Sammy be Richard? I don't think so."

"Or the white one be Dean Martin?"

"Gene be Dean? That doesn't sound right." He said genuinely as if he didn't know the famous duo's of Gene Wilder and Richard Pryor or Dean Martin and Sammy Davis Jr.

"Never mind. I like their names." There was no reason to put reason into Abe at this moment in his life. "I hope they will be safe. Do you think there are any Brooklyn foxes?"

"Alex, there are plenty of Brooklyn foxes."

"Of course, it all makes sense. It's a part of nature. The chickens kill the beetles, the foxes kill the chickens, and the high rent kills the foxes."

That weekend I was telling a regular at Brooklyn Ale House all about the chickens. A lady sitting by herself and drinking red wine asked, "Did you say you have chickens and foxes in Brooklyn?"

"And beetles. Don't forget the beetles."

"You serious?"

"Mostly." I said. "My landlord has started a chicken farm in our backyard."

"Amazing." She said with the glass close to her lips. "I have to get out here more often."

"Where did you hail from?"

"All the way from Chelsea."

"Chelsea, England?"

"No that neighborhood across the East River."

"Oh, all the way over there." I said sarcastically. "What brings you out here to farm country?"

"I'm an art dealer. I came to see a gallery opening over on Kent."

"How was it?"

"Raw. Good but raw. Some promising artists."

"But?" I asked because you could tell she was trying to be nice.

"Well in my business you always hope to find that one special artist that no one has ever seen. Grab them before anyone else, and exploit them of course. But this showing didn't have that."

"You know that special artist you talk of? Well, that very well could be my friend George Henri."

"No offense, but you know how many people tell me about their friend the great artist."

"Yeah I bet, but I'm dead serious. I have never seen such a collection of paintings in my life. And the best part for someone like you is that no one else has seen them. Trust me, if they have, you would have heard of him by now."

"What's his name again?"

"George Henri."

"No, you're right, I haven't heard of him. But it's a good name."

I topped off her wine. "That's on me."

"Look at you. You know how to work it." She said. "Not such a farm boy."

"I don't know what you're talking about Miss. Just buying the pretty lady a drink."

"Alright-alright, don't lay it on too thick." She reached in her bag and pulled out her business card. "You're not going to waist my time are you?"

"I'm telling you, you are going to be wowed."

When I told George Henri about this he went into a panic. He asked about a million questions mostly repeating the same question. "What does she want?"

"Just to see your work, to see if she wants to put you in a gallery. That's what people like her do right?"

"Yeah." He said fading off. Like many people in our position, George Henri was afraid of the next step. Creating the art was the easy part. It was what we loved to do no matter how hard and useless it actually seemed to others. And it was also easy to dismiss the system that lead to success. That step toward possible success was like standing on a ledge and looking down. To jump or not to jump?

I set a time for Hestia the art dealer to go by George Henri's loft. It was at 6pm so I got there an hour early to help George out. He was completely shit-faced.

"What did you take?"

"A little of this, a little of that." He said with a distant tragic smile.

I got him a big cup of water. "Here down this."

"Why? I don't need to talk to her."

"Not completely. But I think you want to present yourself as someone serious about your work."

"You can't be serious and fucked up at the same time?"

"I don't know, but I guess what's done is done." I gave him a big hug and then got us both a beer. "I guess I'll just keep this train running."

Hestia arrived right on time.

"So this is George Henri. He's been drinking a little today and would rather not participate in any casual conversations."

"Sure. Nice to meet you George." Then she went to work. I could tell she was excited as soon as she came in and saw the hundreds of pieces all over the room.

"If you need me to move anything let me know." I went to the other side of the loft by the window and had a cigarette. George Henri lit a joint. Hestia took longer than I thought she would. She studied singular pieces for minutes at a time. It definitely seemed she was into it. About an hour later she came over to me. George Henri was fading in and out.

"So I've decided that I can't do anything with this collection."

I was shocked. "Really? That's surprising. Wouldn't you know that after just a few minutes?"

"Usually, but he has an unusual talent that I wanted to find something of use in. But unfortunately there's nothing exceptionally original. He's mastered all the great styles in history, and it's good, it's really good, but I didn't see anything in here that is him, that is that shy drunk odd guy I met when I came in here. That's why I kept searching around the pieces, trying to find that identity that others, others with money would be attracted to."

"I'm not odd!" George Henri opened his eyes and then shut them again.

"I'm sorry I can't do anything. You didn't waste my time though. I think he could be very talented once *he* comes out in his brush." Then she left. I felt like I let George Henri down. I left him there passed out, passed out with a sad expression over his face.

We were all hacks in some way. The information was out there, the sound waves of the past were out there, the ghost's ideas passed from mouth to mouth, from page to page, from computer to computer, and we captured it all, unabashedly mixing it up and calling it our own. That part was true as much as the part about us wanting to create something beautiful and meaningful. It was disheartening, but we must move on, move forward and prove them wrong.

That night I went to Spuyten Duyvil, but Delbert wasn't there. Everyone was gone, all philosophy was missing, only heat left over. I went bar to bar trying to find these things, trying to find Nicolette, Delbert, music, anything to help the emptiness.

George Henri went to the ledge and tried to jump. It didn't work out. No one was there to catch him.

At some point during the night he began washing down pills with a bottle of whiskey.

I was outside 99 when this was happening. The Haitian was outside of East River Bar doing his usual screaming act. He aggressively came toward me and I hurried inside.

At some point during the night George Henri began lighting his paintings on fire one by one, and then dropping them out his window.

Castor was upstairs in 99. I told him that the crazy Haitian was outside again. "Let's just nip this in the bud." He said as if the last straw was three straws before. We went downstairs to defend our block.

At some point during the night George Henri collapsed of an overdose amongst the paintings on fire.

I had the Haitian pinned against a brick wall. He wouldn't listen to reason, he decided to use force as his argument, so I attacked back. I punched him in the head until he fell unconscious.

At some point during the night the fire department came to put out the loft fire and rescue George Henri.

Castor and I left the body of the Haitian on the sidewalk unsure if he was dead or just knocked out. My hand was broken, the bone sticking up inside my skin.

At some point during the night in the hospital, our friend George Henri slipped into a coma.

That same early morning I sat in the emergency room, waiting to get my broken hand looked at while unbeknownst to me, George Henri fought for his life just a floor above.

All of this in one night, all of this destruction in one night. Maybe that was the opposite of gentrification? Maybe that's why everyone looked negatively toward gentrification? We were self destructive by nature. Fighting it was just as perverse as fighting anything else.

CHAPTER 16

FAMILY

WHEN I got back to 99 that morning the Haitian was gone and my hand was still in bad shape. The doctor told me I could have surgery for a large sum of money or let it heal for no money. For the price of nothing, I would forever have a lump on top of my hand, a reminder of that night, a reminder of defending my territory. I went upstairs to go pass out, but before I made it to the bed Abe yelled for me to come into his office. My first thoughts were that he was going to tell me the Haitian was killed last night.

"Your friend George Henri might be dead." He told me. "His building was on fire last night. They took him to New York Methodist hospital."

I must have been in shock because I asked, "What about the Haitian? Have you heard anything?" As if I didn't even hear him say anything about George Henri. There was even the possibility that I expected this to happen.

"No. Castor said you knocked him out."

I stood there for another minute, just staring out the balcony. "Where's Castor?"

"He already went to the hospital."

"Oh, thanks." I finally came out of the trance, and hurried back to the hospital. Castor was in George Henri's room just staring at him. Then Nicolette came in right after me.

It had been almost two months since I had seen her. She looked at the floor until getting to the bed. Then she talked to us while looking at George Henri. I told them what happened with the art dealer.

"You shouldn't have left him alone." Nicolette said.

"I didn't leave him alone. He was passed out when I left."

"Nicolette, you should shut your stupid mouth." Castor said calmly. "Don't come rushing in here like you all of a sudden give a fuck."

Nicolette left the room crying. I looked over at Castor.

"What? It's true, and don't say you disagree."

"Alright, but... I don't know."

We stayed for most of the day. The doctor asked us if we had any family information for George Henri. We didn't know anything about each other families except the generalities. We told the doctor that all we knew was that he was from New Orleans. We didn't know about his family, we didn't know about any of our families. It wasn't anything that was ever brought up. I hadn't talked to my mom since the last Thanksgiving. It was nothing she did, she was a saint, but that's just the way it had to be to mentally get by. Family was something that we would deal with later. In those days we had each other. The doctor took our information and said he would be in touch if anything changed in George's condition.

My hand would take at least eight weeks to become hard and functional. In the meantime I was preparing for a meeting with a literary agent that responded to my novel query letter. It turns out I was preparing for all the wrong things. While I was busy studying every aspect of my book, I apparently should have been preparing my marketing plan. Who would have known you have to be an artist and a schemer also? I met the agent at Housing Works Bookstore on Crosby Street. There was a café with lots of small tables scattered around the store. We got some coffee, said some initial pleasantries, found a table, and then he dropped the bomb on me.

"What do you want to do with this book?" He asked me point blank.

I stared down the end of the barrel and went into stricken confusion. I had never thought about what I wanted to do with the book. I assumed I would write it, get it into someone's hands that could spread it over the world, and then write another book in the meantime. I probably could have said this and it would have sufficed as an answer, but as so many times in school when I was unprepared I answered, "I don't know."

Then the very professional agent went into his very professional spiel about the elements that he would have to deal with and subsequently what I would have to deal with. He took my manuscript, told me if he had time he would go over it, and then he abruptly stood up to shake my hand farewell. But before I shook his hand, my mouth vomited out these words, "I just want to be heard!"

This stopped him in his professional tracks. He put his hand down. Several of the people around the tables in the café stopped what they were doing to watch one of my most embarrassing moments.

"Well Alex, that is naively honest, and I appreciate that, but in order to be heard, you will need an audience that will listen, and I can tell you right off the bat that this book judging by the title, *The Arrogance of Uselessness* is the first thing that will close ears. You have to figure out how you're going to get them to listen and then deliver the words you have to say. That's just how it works." This time he didn't offer a handshake. "I'll be in touch."

Of course he never got in touch. His assistant emailed me to ask if I wanted them to shred my manuscript for free or send it back to me at my cost. Unlike my hand, this time I took the expensive version. My hand gets neglected, but my words get the royal treatment.

When my manuscript finally made it back a week later I took it to Delbert for his advice.

"The Arrogance of Uselessness?" He read the cover page out loud. "What a great title."

"Thank you." I said in relief. I wrote the title before I even started the book. It was what the book was based around. If the title was gone, then I might as well let those assholes shred it.

"How is your friend?"

"George Henri is the same. The doctor said that if he didn't come out of the coma in the first few days then it's not a good sign."

"That's too bad. He's a good kid."

"Yeah. They found his parents. They're at the hospital with him now. We can't go over there, because of course they blame his friends."

"I should go over. They can blame me. I'm the one that told him to set his work on fire."

"No, you told him he should be willing to burn everything, not set his building on fire while ingesting massive loads of drugs."

"Well either way, I would like to go have a talk with him."

CHAPTER 17

GOD

DELBERT walked into the room where George Henri waited to live again. His parents had to go back to Louisiana for a night, so we all were able to be there. Nicolette was softer than normal, ready to come back. She slipped me a note when I walked in the room. It read: MEET ME AT THE ABBEY AT MIDNIGHT? PLEASE?

She did say please, so I wrote back to her on the same piece of paper. BE CAREFUL NOT TO TOUCH THE WALL, THERE'S A BRAND NEW COAT OF PAINT.

She smiled in relief as she read the words. Castor could see something going on, but for once didn't make a sarcastic remark.

Delbert stood beside George Henri. The facts that followed were as unbelievable as just about anything that Delbert had done so far. People without limits to surprise shouldn't be called people.

"Do you want us to leave?" I asked this entity titled Delbert Peach, who was now leaning over George's still body.

"No, I'm just trying to see if he is awake. I don't want to waste his time if he's sleeping, plus I don't want to wake him. If there's anything I truly hate is being woken up from a nap before I'm ready."

We all agreed with that.

Delbert touched his wrist and then started to talk to George Henri as if they were a couple guys sitting at the bar. "Let me just say first of all that sometimes people get confused about what art is. They are given insight and talent by God, and they follow through with these gifts. Then the modern world conspires to ruin the meaning of those gifts. When the world was young and humans were just learning how to use art, it was useful in the way that if someone wanted to see the sun at night, an artist could draw or paint the sun and it made sense. Art imitating life and such.

"When I saw God on the F-Train it was apparent right away that he was upset. I looked around at what he was looking at. Every person in that train car was occupying their time with some sort of electronic device. It was as if everything he had made was obsolete, everything except the human that invented these distractions. It would be as if you created a painting that encouraged the observer to look at anything but the painting. I followed God around after he got off at the Broadway stop. He watched his world moving on without him. After a while of following him and observing his disappointment I approached God and asked him if he knew which way Central Park was. God looked at me and told me that I knew which way Central Park was. 'It's true.' I told him. 'I just couldn't think up anything else to break the ice.'

'Is there something I can do for you?' He asked.

'I've been watching you for a couple of hours now, watching what you were watching and I couldn't help but notice your disappointment.'

'Yes. It seems me and my creations have become useless. There's no point in fighting against technology anymore.'

'That doesn't sound right. Every day you have the ability to get up and create life. That has to be the most rewarding ability ever.'

'It used to be, but it seems no one appreciates it any more.'

'Well isn't this your world? The only thing you have to do is follow the passion that you get when creating and let what happens outside of that go and take its own path. That was the original point right?'

"God smiled at me and walked away. Computers can create an image of the sun, can be programmed to write a poem or a song, to create a sculpture, but the computer can't feel joy and accomplishment, or be enlightened by its creation. This modern world can't change how one feels about their creations. It's easy to get down about your art when you count on other's attention. But this is your world George Henri. All you have to do is create and breathe, and whatever happens outside of that can take its own path. Okay?" He waited for a few seconds. "Alright, good talk." Then Delbert left without saying anything else. He gave us all a wave by his hip as if he was trying to hide it.

"Was that weird?" Nicolette asked us.

"No." I said. "We all should be talking to George Henri. It's supposed to be good for him I think."

"I'll read him a poem."

"That's my cue to leave." Castor said.

"Jerk." Nicolette punched him in the arm.

"Good to have you around gal." Castor gave her a hug.

At midnight I walked into the Abbey Bar and found an empty table in the back. Nicolette came in a few minutes later. She ordered two beers and two shots, and brought them back to the table. Then she put two yellow pills beside the beers. We did the shots, chased it with the pills, and then chased it with the beers; our eyes locked the whole time like a couple of card sharks. She looked away first.

"You know I'm never like this." She said. "I don't like being like this. I don't want to be like this. I've been like this since that night."

I didn't know what to say, so I didn't say anything.

"I wanted to know what dying feels like."

"I'm not following, you wanted to commit suicide?"

"No, I just wanted the feeling. If I died then everything disappears with me, so instead of dying, I just made everything I know disappear."

"And I'm everything?"

"Yes, you are everything in many ways, but I mean more of everything I knew before when I was on that path, that misguided path."

"Remember the first words you said to me on that rooftop, the night we met?"

"Um... I don't remember a lot about that night."

"You told me and George Henri that we wouldn't be lonely this year."

"Right. I did say that."

"Well, now you have been going out of your way to be nothing but lonely."

"I see where you're going buddy."

"Do you?" I said. "I mean from what you have told me, you've never not been lonely. I think you don't know how to not be lonely."

"Alright-alright, stop analyzing me. I'm trying to figure things out, and you're probably right, but I'm here now, I'm trying now." She quickly leaned over and kissed me.

"You should have just told me that before." I joked.

"That's the beauty. I didn't know that before. That's what I was figuring out. At the time I had the knot in my brain and the only way to untie it was to act irrationally. I just wanted to be corrupted, you know. I wanted my system to be reset. I wanted to wake up feeling hate and corruption. I thought that would cure me of being this way."

"Is that a new poem?"

"I'm not joking. I know it sounds like a little rebellious girl thing to say, but I don't know what else to do. I can't give in to it, not now, I'm too young."

"What about me is so threatening to keep you locked away in a fence. I can corrupt you just as much as anything else."

"No you can't."

It was true.

"You're everything I want, but everything that will make me comfortable. And I can't be comfortable, not now, maybe not ever."

"Don't worry Nicolette, I'm just going to lock you in a book, not a picket fence."

"I love you Alex."

"Damn, I didn't see that coming." I said. "Fuck off Nicolette. You're not going to mind fuck me."

"Then what about the other way?"

Goddamn women.

I grabbed her hand and took her to the bathroom. I let her mind fuck me, and also the other way. Afterward, we walked up the Williamsburg Bridge holding hands, talking about how that night would be the last time we would do this. We would go back to being friends, go back to being a writer and a poet. Love and sex would not ruin what we came to New York for. On our left was the greatest skyline in the world, and on our right was the greatest neighborhood in the world. We simply stared out over both entities, hand in hand, back on the same team.

On the way back down the bridge, Nicolette got a phone call from an unknown number. She answered it. "Hello?"

"Hello. Nicolette? It's me, George Henri."

CHAPTER 18

THE THIEF

JUST hours after Delbert had come in to have a talk with George Henri, his eyes opened, his fingers moved back and forth, and the feeling in his legs came back. He said it all just felt like a short sleep. He remembered having a dream about God on the subway, and then he woke up just like any other day, but this time he understood something bigger than a regular wakening. "My eyes opened and for the first time I knew why they opened. There's no way I could explain it to you or anyone else, but I think I can find it on the canvas. I can't explain it, but I think I can paint it." George Henri was arrested for arson as soon as he got out of the hospital and eventually sentenced to a drug rehabilitation facility until administration felt he was ready for a sober life. He was there for seven weeks in which he spent every single free minute painting.

"I saw the vision in my coma and it just took over my hand." He told us. "It was easy as breathing." His new work was nothing like he had done before. I didn't know if it was better or worse than what he was doing before, but it was definitely original.

We never told him about Delbert's visit and conversation in the hospital. We were afraid that it would jinx his new understanding.

I told all this to Delbert and he seemed deliriously surprised and happy. "Isn't that wonderful. Life can be so surprising and magical." He told me.

I also told him about Nicolette, how we were just going to be friends and it was going to be painful, but we decided worth it. He agreed. "Reaching that point of not looking back is the closest thing we have to defying death."

"Didn't I say that in my book?"

"I'm not sure, it is possible, I rarely have a completely original thought."

I asked if he had read my book, and he said that he had finished it the first night that I gave it to him.

"I love that title." He commented.

He had *The Arrogance of Uselessness* in his possession for weeks now and had said nothing about it. That gave me reservations about asking him about it. "Yes, you have said that before."

"I don't pride myself on repetition, but in this case I'll allow it, because I really love that title."

"The pride."

"Yes, I give myself rations of pride, a half-full canteen in the desert."

"Is there anything else that you can maybe think about the book?" I was beating around the bush as they say.

"I thought many things about your book."

Sometimes I was uncertain if he didn't finish sentences on purpose or if the thought was complete. "So I guess that's better than not having any thoughts huh?"

"Alex, I have to clarify because we've already seemed to go through this with your friends, do you want art advice, or life advice?"

I tried to recall the formula that he told me before, which was life advice can ruin one's art, and art advice can ruin one's life. I had no choice but to take a chance on ruining my life. As far as I was concerned, that was all I had. Writing was my life. That part was easy.

"I want your most honest opinion on the book, and I want your most honest advice on how I can make it better?" I said with a lump in my throat.

"You know what I thought mostly? I thought this guy, this author, you, I thought that you need to learn how to be better thief."

"Excuse me?"

"There were just too many times that I caught you with your hand in someone's pocket, too many times in which you returned a wallet that you found on the ground."

"I know you're trying to say something to me here, and I'm sure it's important but… not getting it."

"Come on. I'll show you." He chugged the rest of his beer and we headed out of the bar. When we got outside, he showed me a wine opener. "See. Just snaked this off the bar. Later on tonight the bartender will possibly look around for this if he needs it and eventually find another way to open the bottle. If he doesn't need it, he'll probably just forget about it all together."

"Okay. Are we going to stick someone up now?"

"Yes, now you're thinking!"

I was a little afraid that he was serious. He led me to an abandoned building on Grand that is now one of those giant multiplex movie theaters. "Our old friend." He said and pointed to a wall full of graffiti. One of the tags was the ever-familiar dollar sign. This one read: LIFE IS WHAT YOU STEAL$.

Then he took me to Rosemary's Tavern on Bedford. We apparently were going to steal every wine-key in the city. He saddled up on a stool at the bar and took out a notebook. "That's it. Get your notebook out." I followed his lead. "Write down character number one." He ordered us two beers. "Now it's time to start taking shit." Delbert took a deep breath and motioned for me to do the same.

An old drunk in a booth laughed out loud.

"Take it." Delbert told me.

"Take what?"

"That laugh. Grab it and hide it away." He pointed to the page on my notebook. Then I saw what he was getting at. "See the bartender's big drooping ass? Take it." I wrote it down. "See that used bar napkin over there. Take it." I started to write it down, but he stopped my pen. "No. Take it. Grab it. Hold it in your hand. Smell it. Take it home with you."

"That's just weird."

There was a couple at the bar in a deep conversation. He asked her, "Do you still love me?" And she replied, "I don't know."

Delbert with a big grin whispered to me, "Oh my, definitely steal that. What a gem!"

We went to the Salvation Army and he made me steal a hideous costume necklace. We went to Surf Bar and he made me steal sand. We went to the waterfront and he made me steal a construction permit. We took a ride on the L-Train and he made me steal a hipster's observation that the "Europeans moving into the neighborhood were driving rent up." We went to Tompkins Square Park and he made me steal drug addicts' chess moves. We took a ride on the J-Train and he made me steal some teenagers' break-dance moves.

"Your book is valid, but it needs less of the things that you've collected, bought, borrowed, and been given. The book is full of obvious personal experiences gone awry in your head. It needs the experiences you have stolen. Make them yours." Then Delbert easily lifted a pink wallet out of a woman's purse. "Writing isn't immaculate conception. You have to take everything you see, hear, feel, run into, imagine, you steal it all Alex… and then you write." He tapped the woman on the shoulder. "Excuse me miss I think you dropped this." The woman took back the wallet while thanking him over and over.

The doors opened on the train at the Marcy stop. He told me to get out. "Time to go out on your own. Every thief for himself from here on out." I stepped off the train, the doors shut, and I looked back because he was knocking on the window. Delbert Peach wore his signature grin in which it seemed like he had just discovered gold. The train started to pull away. In his hand he held high the notebook that he just stole from me.

CHAPTER 19

DOORS AND SUNRISES

THE night George Henri was released from rehab-jail, we all met out at Spuyten Duyvil. Just as George Henri and I went to the hospital on the same night, we had both healed in same amount of time. My hand was back to being fully functional and his life was back to being fully functional. We were talking about this coincidence when Nicolette walked in with her new boyfriend. He was the quintessential hipster that gave the subculture its annoying reputation. He was a graphic designer, a singer songwriter, a keyboard player in his own synth-pop band, a poet, an abstract painter, a polaroid photographer, he smoked Nat Sherman's, he owned a skateboard, he owned a fixed-gear bike, he had a tattoo sleeve consisting mostly of wild animals and obscure film maker's faces, his favorite author was Andre Breton, his favorite band was Destroyer, he knew where to get the best burrito in the city even though it never would be as good as San Francisco, and the topper as always, was that he was unemployed and most likely getting checks from older family bank accounts.

That being said, he was a very nice guy, just the reason why many people including our own had some sort of misdirected disdain for us. Our identity had been placed into a marketable style while we tried to find anything that didn't go along with their marketing studies. There was little left to rebel against. We needed to be a part of something when there was nothing to be a part of, nothing to fight for without a clipboard and brightly colored tee shirt. In the meantime the media was so much faster than our record collections and bohemian ideals. In 2006 we began to lose the race.

I had talked to Delbert about these minor inconveniences and he thought that our generation was the tortoise and this invisible worldwide communication system was the hare. "The tortoise will beat the hare." He reassured us that night. "You are the first generation that will be able to take your art and take control of it yourself. Finally you don't have to wait for some out-of-touch corporate suit to tell you what you're worth, to tell you whether or not the masses will get to see what they think as being worthy of being seen, or heard, or felt.

You will still have these reservations about what success is and you will wonder if it counts if it's done in your hands or in the hands of those who are known to validate. No matter what I tell you about how we are programmed to be successful and how all you need to do is satisfy the reasons you started to do the creative work in the beginning, those questions will linger until later generations are reprogrammed. I suppose if the reason was to be successful then that would be justified, but either way bringing it in the light won't make it go away. Being there makes it go away, being successful brings it fully in the light, and its image is comical. At your frontal lobe rests your own version of success. At your fingertips rests your future. What do they call it?" He wasn't necessarily asking us, but himself. He thought hard for a minute. "D.I.Y. Do it yourself. You will be the first cohesive do-it-yourself generation."

We passed around our whiskey flask. George Henri was so happy to have booze in his system. "Sobriety is not for me thank you. It's time to live!"

We had never seen him like this. He was vibrant, confident, and almost what one would call sexual. We all knew he was gay, but he never talked about it or acted upon it. The new George Henri let it all hang out. It made the group closer and easier with each other.

"That's right George Henri." Delbert said. "It is time to live. Go out and show them your passion! Do not wait on them!"

I got chills as everyone else slipped through the seconds. That portable second was the future. I saw it without the telescope. We were to take hold of our lives, take hold of our art, and leave the old regime way up high in their towers to silently fade away.

Then Nicolette's date took away my chills.

"Hey. You know what we should do? We should start a zine!"

"A what?" Castor asked.

"A zine. An art zine with photos and art and stories and Nicolette's poems. That would be rad."

Even though it wasn't a horrible idea, it was exactly what someone like him would say. It would be perfect to add to his resume of everything and nothing at the same time. I had always been suspicious of those who wore too many hats.

"Yeah rad. Let's do it." I said sarcastically and Nicolette loved me for it.

He kept rambling on about what we could do with our zine, but we would never hang out with him again, and his words fell short as every watered-down activity in his life would. As he talked I thought about what Delbert had said. I thought about putting together an event for us, a gathering that would represent us, our little group trying to be heard, the first push of the fight.

Before Nicolette and her new boyfriend left, she came running back to me.

"Hey, it's great to be a part of this again. It's great to hear your voice, see your face. Sorry I'm such a selfish brat." She held on to my elbow. "Whenever I grow out of it, I hope you'll still be around." She kissed me on the cheek purposely catching the corner of my lips. I think I even felt a tear catch in between our cheeks. "And thanks for putting up with him."

"That part is easy. He's… nice. I'm sure you'll ruin him."

CHAPTER 20

XAVIER NASHAK

THE autumn had come and we were all settling into this new mentality of taking control of our work. Connor had a sound proof studio put in his loft and The Secrets were recording their first LP. George Henri had found a tall and handsome man with a large work studio to share. Nicolette was making chap books from her thousands of poems. I had been working on a new novel that was pouring out, because I hadn't been able to write with my lame hand. It had been building up for weeks while I wrote down vaguely decipherable notes with my left hand.

It was a Monday night when I had finished the first handwritten draft of my new book. I went to have a beer with Delbert and tell him all about it. This would be the last time I would ever see him. Of course I didn't know that at the time, but I did feel that there was something about our patron saint of Williamsburg that had maybe finished what he had come to do. He was just as angelic as always, but he also seemed hesitant to expand on his thoughts. Delbert always had the ability to take the simplest subject a little further than anyone I had ever met, but that night he stopped short on everything from Lambic beers to the C.C.R. playing over the crackly speakers.

As I told him about the book, he responded as if he already had read it. "The direction is good, but the direction will soon change. It will make itself apparent, probably very very soon." He said slowly while looking across the room.

"I don't know if I can handle cryptic criticism tonight."

He kept looking across the room. There was a man down the bar that seemed to keep looking at us. I thought I saw Delbert giving him the inquisitive-eye earlier in the night. The man got up from his bar stool and walked over to us. The man had an unsure smile on his face as he proclaimed, "Xavier? Xavier Nashak?"

Delbert remained quiet until saying, "I'm sorry, but are you talking to me?"

"Yes, of course. It's Mike, Michael Bauer from Buffalo. We went to St. Joseph's High together."

"Once again, I'm sorry, but you have the wrong person. I'm from Cheyenne, Wyoming, and I never went to high school."

Michael Bauer looked at him closely while holding a waiting expression as if Delbert was screwing around with him. "Well boy, you sure do look and sound just like Xavier Nashak to me. Boy do I feel like a monkey's asshole. Sorry to bother you."

"No bother, me and my friend had lost a subject to talk about anyway. Now, we will talk about this. Thank you."

"See, that's just something Xavier would say. Always able to turn every damn thing into a slice of heaven."

"Sounds like a wonderful fellow."

"I suppose. I haven't seen him since he disappeared right before graduation." Michael took one last look at Delbert. "Alright, once again sorry to bother you."

After he went back to his spot down the bar, Delbert said, "I guess I just have one of those faces."

"Have you ever been to Buffalo?"

"Buffalo?" He thought about something, but it didn't seem like it was whether he had been to Buffalo or not. "I just remembered that I have to go." He stood up. "I thought I needed to be here for something, but I don't." Then he left without looking at me. I thought it was strange, but beyond all the glory and saintliness of Delbert Peach he was at heart, a very strange man. So I didn't think anything about it, until I started to leave and Michael Bauer got my attention.

"That man you were with, who is he?"

"Delbert Peach."

"Delbert Peach, Delbert Peach. I know that name from somewhere." He said. "I tell you though, if there was a twin for my high school friend Xavier Nashak, he was the one. The voice and everything."

"You said that he disappeared. What happened?"

"Just a couple weeks before graduation Xavier took off. He left a note for his parents that said something about how no piece of paper would ever make him a poet, about how no friends or family would make him a poet. No one really understood, because he had never written a single poem as far as anyone knew."

I lied to Michael Bauer. I told him that that statement didn't sound anything like Delbert Peach even though it's exactly something he had told me before. I figured if Delbert didn't want to be Xavier any longer, then no one should ask him to be.

I went home to 99 and got on Abe's computer. I searched the name 'Xavier Nashak,' but nothing significant came up. I searched the name 'Delbert Peach' and most of the hits had something to do with actual peaches. Then the name came up in some book forum website. I clicked on the site and it had a list of characters from a Kurt Vonnegut book called *God Bless You Mr. Rosewater*. Then I looked up the book and found out that Delbert Peach was the town drunk in the story. His brief appearance was highlighted by this conversation piece:

'I'm leaving,' said Peach. 'I know when I'm not wanted.'

'I imagine you've had plenty of opportunities to learn,' said the Senator.

Of course Delbert would choose his alias to be the most pathetic character in a book. While everyone else is out there naming their kids after sports stars and rock stars, while everyone else out there is relating their names to Greek and Roman Gods, while everyone else out there desires to be the smartest, the fastest, the tallest, Delbert Peach is in a bar in Williamsburg just waiting for the last woman standing to take him home. Sometimes she does, sometimes she doesn't. Delbert once told me, 'Women have the uncanny ability to distinguish between unconsciousness and indifference from across a crowded bar. Both have worked in my advantage.'

That line gave me an idea.

I began searching the Internet for everything that Delbert had told me. There had to be something more to this mysterious man. After an hour or so I typed in, 'God F-Train' because of that story he told George Henri while in a coma. One of the hits that came up was called *God on the F-Train.*

It was a story in the New Yorker from Xavier Kahsan, a writer that was notorious for his elusiveness from the media. At the time, many of the kids in the neighborhood were taking in the resurgence of this author from two decades ago. Xavier Kahsan had disappeared from existence about as fast as he came on. As matter of a fact he never really even *came on*. From the very beginning when he released his only three books in as many years, no one actually ever saw him. He never did readings, he never had his picture taken, and he had yet to be described by anyone that knew him from the past. All his books were considered before their time. They were definitely before many things, including the Internet and the mass media that can't be escaped any longer.

His most popular novel was called *Generation Distracted*. It was huge success, gaining a cult following at first, then it broke through to the mainstream, and then it went out of print until around that time of 2006. The rumor was that it was written by one of the other famous recluse writers under a pen name. The experts guessed that it was J.D. Salinger, because of the ridiculously witty style and the simple yet priceless insight, but the author had never been revealed until that moment sitting in 99 South 6th Street on a warm September night.

I wasn't even sure to do with the information, because I loved our dynamic. If I told him I knew then it would ruin that relationship. Turns out that wouldn't matter. I spent the next week checking into Spuyten Duyvil, but Delbert wasn't in his position.

After a few days I asked the regular bartender there about Delbert.

"Who?"

"You know Delbert. The man that usually sits on this stool every day of the week."

"Oh you mean, Henry." He replied

"Henry?"

"Yeah, Henry. Henry, something Polish, ski something."

Then I described Delbert and he agreed with all the detail.

"Not Henry Chinaski?" I asked about his name.

"Yeah, I think that's it."

Henry Chinaski was Charles Bukowski's alter ego that also was a pathetic drunk. I knew all of a sudden that all of Xavier Nashak's life was stolen. He was the greatest thief that may have ever lived. He stole his whole life.

I decided to get bold, because after having this information for a week or so I had to talk to someone about it. Delbert was the only person I could actually talk to, so I went to the Domino's Sugar plant to find him. The logical start was at that spilt in the chain-link fence. On the other side was a rocky and trashed up space between the buildings. Above that alley were two giant shoots that connected the buildings. I imagined that at some point in time, billions of grains of sugar poured through those shoots, and now just stale air, rats, and spiders occupied the connections. The night I followed Delbert, he had gone to the back of the opening and I'm pretty sure that he went inside around the old docking area. I went back to that area and stood on the platform overlooking the Manhattan skyline. One day real estate vampires would fight over this forgotten property, but then it was just one man hiding from the world in between 14 million people.

There was a padlock on the shutter door that wasn't closed. I took it off and lifted the sliding door. It was dark inside with rays of the late sun piercing through partially unblocked windows. I scaled through the rubble and debris until getting to where Delbert had to be living. There was a piano and a hammock blocked off by piles of used office furniture. I can't even begin to fathom where, much less how he got a piano into the building. There was also a desk and a swivel chair. On the desk was a letter weighted down by his Belgian Lambic glass.

Dear Alex,

I assumed at some point you would figure it out before anyone else. It was a good run. It always is, but they always find you. We can do this for days, sometimes years at a time, but they will always smell you out and then you have to keep moving to that next piece of holy ground. I will see you there and have a different name, a different face, but I will have the same voice. You will know it when you hear it.

Your friend,

Delbert Peach

When I came out of the old sugar factory, the first thing I saw was the construction of the two new condominium towers and I realized what Delbert was talking about. They will always find you. 2006 was a special year and I had to finish what I had come for. They were coming and I had to get it ready for them.

CHAPTER 21

SHANTYTOWN

WHEN I walked out onto South 6th Street the chickens were roaming the sidewalks like some hipsters hanging out on the corner. Hipster-chickens, the new generation of poultry. I figured they were in search for more metal. They were addicts. We had to clear all the nuts and bolts and any other small pieces of metal from the backyard, because they would eat it. If you had those metal shoelace eyelets they would come peck at your feet. Our chickens had a serious problem.

Seth came out also. He looked down at the freed chickens, said, "Must be looking for metal." and then went on his bodega run. The chickens saw him and for whatever reason started to follow him. I walked behind all of them trying to figure out how I could get them back. Seth turned around and looked at us all with no expression. He said, "It seems as if they were just waiting for something to follow."

Then he kept walking, unconcerned with their freedom. His backpack was slightly open and it looked like there were spray paint cans inside. I never asked what Seth actually did in this world, but I was pretty certain it didn't have anything to do with painting.

I yelled up to Abe on the second floor. He came out while on the phone.

"They're loose!"

"Who?"

"Sammy Davis Jr. and friends."

Abe came down, yelled at them in Hebrew, and they followed him into the backyard. He brought everyone together, no matter what background the chickens were from. I went up to his office and proposed an idea I had been mulling over since that night at Spuyten Duyvil when Delbert told us to take control. "Abe, I want to throw an event, but I need your help, I need your contacts and acquaintances." I told him. "But not just a regular event, I want to this to be loud, I want a concert, a reading, an art opening, a bar, a gathering, a movement captured within a night."

"Okay, I get twenty percent of the door." He said without looking up.

"I wasn't going to charge."

"Movements are started through business."

"I guess we could charge for the booze. How about fifty percent of the bar?"

"Deal." He shook my hand. "Just let me know when and where and I'll make sure the place is filled."

"Thanks Abe." I started to leave, but he caught me.

"Hey, what do you think about this? A recreational vehicle park?"

"RV parks? I think they are great." I didn't think they were great. "Why?"

"I think I'm going to start one. Look at this. Five hundred dollars on eBay." He directed me toward his computer where an old junked up RV was pictured.

"That's great. Where are you going to do it?" I was thinking upstate New York or New Jersey.

"Right here of course."

"Right here, here?"

"Yeah right here ,here. Line this whole block with RV's. With two renters per vehicle, I could make back the cost in one or two month's rent, water hook-ups can come from the backyard, we would only have to move them once a week for street cleaning, or not even move them, just incur the fine as a part of the rent."

"Well, I say if you could get away with that, then it might be one of your best ideas yet."

"Really?" He sounded surprised as if he just came up with these ideas for shock value.

"Really."

That's apparently all he needed. As I was there, he called the owner of the RV and told him he would come pick it up the next day. He held up his hand to keep me from leaving as if he wanted me to see how he followed through with my approval.

Seth was coming back from the bodega when I stepped out for the second time that day. "I guess they found someone to follow." He said.

"I guess they always do, you just hope your leader is as charismatic as Abe."

Seth laughed, something I had yet to see.

"You know Abe is starting a shantytown of RV's on this block?"

"No, but that sounds about right. I guess I should go and see how he's going to afford this venture."

"What do you do Seth? I mean for a job?"

"I'm in finance."

"Like Wall Street?"

"I suppose, big banks, evil empire stuff."

"So why are you living in a secret refrigerator room in Williamsburg?" I tried to not sound pretentious, but it came off that way.

"You know this street connecting with Broadway used to be the second biggest financial district in the country next to Wall Street?"

"No, I had no idea."

"Just look." He brought me over to the other side of the street. "Look at the magnificent buildings that all used to be banks."

It was true. I passed by the structures that looked like they could be from ancient Rome everyday without thinking why they were there.

"So that's why you live here, the financial history without the financial bullshit of Manhattan."

"I wouldn't say that. I just like being somewhere interesting."

People around Williamsburg liked to talk about gentrification, liked to put down the new condos that were soon to be built, liked to hate on the new bars and restaurants that would eventually open every week, but if it could be put into the simplest terms like Seth just did, then it's hard to join in on the lynch mob. People just want to be somewhere interesting, people want to open up bars where interesting people will come to, and yes, big businesses want to build condos where they can sell this ideal to people with money that want to live somewhere that is interesting. It's not ideal, but it will always be that way. Just as Delbert Peach had to go find the next place where condos would break ground, so would anyone else who still loved to defy mainstream currents running through what used to be interesting. It's not a new concept, and it will always be that way. The mainstream will always latch on to the interesting and find a way to water it down enough so everyone can enjoy it.

Before Seth went inside I told him, "You know I saw something that reminded me of you the other day."

"Oh yeah?"

"Yeah, I was looking through the telescope and way up on the top floor of that building over there on Bedford and Broadway, you can't see it right now, but you can see it through the telescope. Someone had spray painted WE LIVE IN REFRIGERATORS, LIFE PRESERVED UNTIL ITS DUE DATE$. And it was punctuated with a dollar sign."

"Yeah, that does sound like me." He smiled and went inside. All of a sudden Seth made a lot more sense.

Later that night I went out to the telescope and turned it toward the bridge. There was a young Puerto Rican man up there that I had seen before. He always had a 40oz of Bud and he always had big earphones on. Sometimes he smoked weed and danced, and he was always peaceful. Through the telescope lens I could see into his eyes. He seemed content up there with his beer and music and view. He seemed like he didn't need anyone to follow. There was a little bit of everything here in Williamsburg, even people that didn't care if they were around somewhere interesting.

CHAPTER 22

THE GIRL WITH SMALL HANDS

I went to Spoonbill & Sugartown Bookstore on Bedford and bought all three of Xavier Kahsan's novels. They were very popular at that moment, risen from the out-of-print ashes like the Phoenix of literature. Two weeks later I had finished them all with a giant grin on my face. If I would have read these at the beginning of the year, I would have known right away that Delbert and Xavier were one in the same. Everything he had ever told me was woven in the pages of his books. But if I had known, then it would have ruined everything.

He was the last great literary novelist of the big publisher days, the one who didn't need to be marketable, the one who didn't have to fool the public into buying trash. The great authors of today are judged on how well the movie adaption sells. No one could make a movie out of Delbert's books, the language doesn't translate, the emotion isn't actable, and the bliss can't be digitized. Delbert or Xavier or whoever he is tomorrow, he will be missed, never forgotten.

When I walked out of 99 to go to work, the shantytown was in its budding stages. There were four RV's parked outside of 99 along with a band of New England hipster gypsies hanging out on the sidewalk. They were all shirtless and dirty and shifty-eyed. They smoked and drank and gambled and wrestled and yelled at their wild dogs. This is just what the neighborhood needed, the opposite of gentrification. They would be begging for the condo-dwellers after Abe got done with the South 6th Street shantytown. I headed to work, making sure to say hello to all my new neighbors. If nothing else, I could be hospitable.

Saturday nights at the Ale House were becoming a big shit-show. I suppose it was a perfect place to be on an autumn evening in Brooklyn. It was good for me because I finally after a couple of years felt like I was a little bit ahead financially. Not eating was always easy, but not drinking could cause slight anxiety, and not drinking and not having rent at the end of a month was just plain sickening. Luckily I was making money, eating free snacks, and drinking free beer all in the same place, all the wonderful components of my particular survival under one roof.

The bar began to empty out around 3am when she walked in. *She* had jet-black hair against pale creamy skin, huge light blue eyes, a tendency to look away when I tried to eye her from afar, and a tendency to lock you in when eyeing her close up. She ordered a white wine. I pretended to be busier than I was because I was actually afraid to talk to her. She finished the first glass of wine quickly. I went over to refill the empty glass. "On me." I said and she didn't seem to understand. She put a twenty-dollar bill out.

I pushed it back, "Just say thank you."

She didn't get my joke or say thank you.

One of our regulars that brought his hound dog Fred in the bar asked me about the girl.

"I don't know." I told him. "But it's just not natural to trust a girl that pretty in a bar by herself at four in the morning."

There was this shelf by the bar that held a dozen old books, nothing to really read, but more for aesthetics and for the occasional bored girl to pass the time while finishing a glass of wine. She reached up to take off *The Collective Works of Mark Twain*. I've always been attracted to small hands taking big books off of shelves. I told her that and she finally smiled. It was an awkward smile, like she wasn't use to doing it.

Paige was wasted at closing time, so she left me on my own to shut down. It was just me, the girl, and the regular with his hound dog Fred. I kept refilling the girl's glass and she kept putting a twenty-dollar bill out while locking me in her stare. I was beating around the bush as they say.

"You two look like you're in love with each other." The regular said.

"Thanks for making things a little more awkward."

"Just saying, you two can't keep your eyes off each other."

"Once again. Thanks. You about done? I need to lock the door."

The girl started to get up.

"Not you." I put my hand on top of her fingers.

"Is this when you're supposed to say, if you're not screwing the bartender then you got to go home?" She said and laughed at herself.

That's when I figured it out. "You've never done this before have you?"

She understood what I meant. She turned her eyes away from me. "No, I guess not."

The regular finally left with his hound dog Fred. "See you Fred." I locked the door behind them. "If it makes you feel better, I've never done this before either."

"Yes. That does make me feel better." She got up to leave again. "I should leave huh?"

"I don't want you to."

Then she came up to me and hugged me as if I were a lover that she hadn't seen in ten years. When she let go I kissed her. It was like one of those kisses in a movie from the 1930's, hard pressed lips with the slight tilt and dip. I had never done that either. I had never tried to pick up a girl while working at the bar. It was a night of firsts.

I locked up the bar without doing anything. I could come back in the morning and clean up before the noon opening. At that moment, nothing could stop me, not even the idea of going back to not paying rent or eating or drinking.

Goddamn women.

We walked back to 99 holding hands and talking like an old couple. I was just drunk enough to not be scared of the ramifications of this speedy progression.

She asked me under her breath, which turned out to be the only way she spoke, "Do you believe in love at first sight?"

"Believe in it? I believe that it's the only real love there actually is." Even though I was just trying to be witty, as I said those sentimental words, it actually made sense. I didn't really believe that, but I believed that for me at the time.

Then there was a crack of thunder. Then there was a bolt of lightening that struck down over Manhattan. Then the downpour came. We ran till finding shelter under the door overhang of the Levee bar. The rain came down on our feet as we made-out until the drops subsided. By the time we got back to 99 the downpour had started again. I went to unlock the door, but it was already open. We stepped up inside out of the rain and the downstairs open space was filled with gypsy squatters.

"Who are all these people?" She asked me.

"You want the long or short version?"

Most of them didn't even notice me come in, but there was the one ringleader, Dusty that waved at me and explained, "The campers don't hold hard rain that much. We'll get that fixed tomorrow."

"Oh good."

We went upstairs and of course there were more people up there, including two dirty and wet young men waiting on the bathroom. I showed her into my bedroom, and then I went to handle my unwanted guests.

"Hey guys, use the bathrooms in your campers or go outside. I have a guest over. You are not my guests."

They grunted out apologies. Then I went in Abe's office where there were more shitheads on the balcony. "Guys? You can't be up here after dark. Go downstairs or find somewhere else to hang out. Thanks."

"But Abe said we could hang here."

"Abe is not here. I am. I have a friend over and I swear to God if you disturb us even the slightest bit, just once, I'm coming out here with a fucking baseball bat and I'm not going to stop swinging until every single one of you are dead. Now, do you want to call Abe and ask him if you can still hang out in the house that I rent?"

Then Castor appeared behind me with the said baseball bat. "Or we can just start swinging now?" It was just like in the movies when the partner shows up just in time to save the day.

More grunted apologies came as Castor escorted them down the stairs.

Then I went into my bedroom where she waited in bed with her clothes still on. She stared at me nervously like she knew something I didn't.

"What?" I asked her but she didn't answer. She took her hand and felt along the wall where all of my thoughts had been transferred.

"Did you write all this?"

"Yeah, something I do in my sleep."

"Why?"

"Because I couldn't imagine doing anything else. Nothing in this world could compensate the feeling of taking something blank and filling it with words, with life, with stories, with these people."

I pointed to a specific line about my friends. "I've always been surprised, and baffled, and enamored every time I look at the ink-filled pages, or in this case, the walls, and it's as if it happened magically, as if my hand had separated from my body and it went on some wonderful trip." I had never been able to explain my love of writing like that before and I knew that she was the…

She was looking up at me, hanging on every word. I crawled into bed and she wrapped herself around my upper body. We fell asleep in between kissing. It was nice in my room, the temperature was just cold enough to use each other's bodies, there wasn't a peep from the shitheads downstairs, and my words all over the wall were just waiting for the sun to push past my window. We woke up several times throughout the morning and went straight back into kissing. Our clothes were still intact with no intention of changing. For whatever reason our interaction wasn't to be about sex, just about intimacy.

When I woke up for the last time at 11am, realizing that I had to get back to the Ale House to clean, she was reaching up to take a book off my shelf. I watched her carefully read the back cover and then look inside at the first page. It was as beautiful sight as I might have ever seen.

"Have you read it before?"

She shook her head.

"Take it." I was a true believer in the great book exchange, the one that happens all over the world at any given moment.

"Okay." She put *Generation Distracted* in her tote bag. "What's it about?"

"It's about a man trying to save the world from itself, about him learning the impossibility of the task, so he instead goes after the individual, the individual that will make a difference in hopes it will spread like a virus."

"Well don't ruin it."

"You can't ruin it. I could read it another ten times and it would still be just as special."

Then there was an awkward silence, because we knew this was about to end.

"So…I hate to be that guy, but I really have to get back to work to clean before they open."

"Okay." She sounded sad. She abruptly shot over to me and kissed me desperately. I think normally I would mentally retract from this, but since I already knew that it was going to be just a one-night stand of sorts, I kind of liked it. I just kept thinking that I had to do what I would normally not do. Normally I would have just jumped into this seemingly perfect relationship, but I had to stick to my convictions.

"So is this where we exchange numbers and never call each other?" She said.

"Yeah, normally, but I don't have a phone, so I would have to give you a fake number, and I don't want to give you a fake number." I was reaching for the right words but they didn't happen. "I'm at the Ale House every weekend… I mean if you get thirsty… I'm there."

"How about I just give you my number?"

"You can, but… by the time I call you, you'll be married, happy, and probably live in a house upstate, and I'll hate myself for waiting so long, because I really like your voice, and I really like your hands." It might have been the best and worst thing I have ever said to a woman, because it was the truth. I had to keep looking through telescopes during that time. I had no choice.

"Okay," was all she said, head down, the tip of her shoe trying to find a pebble. I walked her to the subway. We held hands all the way there. It wasn't weird. On the corner of Bedford and North 7th we kissed one last time, one last time like the last kiss in a movie from the 1930's.

She told me before walking down the steps, "You're going to finish what you need to finish and then you'll start something new. I'm going to be what's new."

That blindsided me. I stood there dumbfounded by her words as she disappeared into the underground.

CHAPTER 23

MADONNA ARMS

I woke to bass thumping through my bedroom floor. I went to the bathroom to throw some water over my face. The flies had finally gone extinct. There were dead fly corpses scattered in the corners, reminders that the summer had passed. Then I followed the music downstairs until discovering eight women in leotards exercising to house music. The instructor yelled at me to participate or get out, so I got out. On the sidewalk was a chalkboard that read: MADONNA ARMS WORKOUT EVERY TUESDAY AND THURSDAY AT NOON. When I went back inside, I could hear the nasally voice of the instructor saying, "Come on girls! Do you want Madonna arms?"

I gathered my writing tools and my bike, and then headed to Verb Café. The café had become my go-to spot to write. I was superstitious when it came to good or bad streaks. I was on a real ripper the past week, ever since I met that girl with the small hands. It was the kind of one-night stand that artists dream about.

"I thought I'd find you here." Nicolette appeared in front of me. I was in the back of the café hoping that no one would see me whether they knew me or not. That's what people did before mobile phones, they went to places that everyone would know to find them, or places that no one could find them.

"I'm becoming the predictable being I had always been afraid of. What's up?"

"Nothing. You want to get a drink tonight?"

"Maybe. Your boyfriend going to be with us?"

"No, that's way over." She said proudly. "Was he that bad?"

"Not bad, just annoying."

"Alright-alright. Want to hang with Delbert at Spuyten?"

I had yet to tell anyone about the infamous Delbert Peach or Xavier Nashak, hoping that he would just fade away into a distant book cover. "No, let's go somewhere new."

"Whoa, somewhere new! You're breaking free from your nightmare."

Back in the mid 2000's in Williamsburg there were just the ten or so staple bars to go to, then years later out of nowhere a new bar would open weekly, they would stack them low in between bowling alleys, hotels, and Cineplex's. The neighborhood became like the chewing gum isle in a bodega. That night we all met out at one of the staples called Trash Bar.

Castor was at the bar slurring his words and running into tables, but then he would all of a sudden seem coherent. Nicolette and George Henri were exchanging confused glances at Castor's odd behavior. The Secrets had just self-released their first cd. They were panhandling it on the streets, giving it away after other bands' concerts, and most importantly they were selling it on their website. "It's strange." Castor said. "We are selling a lot of copies, and I'm not sure if it's just Connor buying them to make it look like we're selling a lot, or if people are really hearing about it." The latter was the truth. The Secrets after playing 3.3 shows, had a cult following, and music snobs across the country were trying to get their hands on their music. It took a year or so, but The Secrets' debut LP became the biggest selling self-release in history to date.

We were all drinking pretty heavily in celebration. Castor kept going to the bar, whispering to the bartender, and then coming back with what appeared to be a rum and coke.

"Why are you acting weird?" Nicolette finally asked him

"I'm not acting weird, I'm acting drunk."

"What, with your virgin Cuba Libre's?"

"No, I mean I'm acting like I'm drunk."

"What do you mean? Are you practicing for a role?"

"Not really. This is what I figured. You know how we always go out and get drunk and feel so shitty the next day?"

"No." We all said facetiously.

"But really, and you know how we then say we'll never do that again, but the next night we'll do it all over again. The pattern continues right. So I decided that instead of doing that, I'm going to start pretending to get shit-faced."

"Pretending?"

'Yeah, why not? Everyone lies about something, I'm going to lie about being drunk."

"But now we know, and isn't the purpose to fool others around you?"

"I don't care. You can play along or not. I have to believe my real friends would indulge me a little."

This lasted about week before the hard realization that having a hangover is worth getting drunk in real life. That night he would just have to be weird.

I told the guys about my idea to throw a show with The Secrets playing, George Henri's paintings on display, Nicolette and myself doing a reading, and then other artists mixed in. Everyone loved the idea until I told them where I wanted to do it.

"The Domino Sugar factory?" George Henri asked. "Can you do that?"

"I'm not going to ask anyone. I know how to get inside, and there's not anyone around for blocks so no one will figure it out, at least not until it's too late."

They all thought it was a cool idea, but also not very practical.

"I'll set it all up. We could make fliers with specific directions to the factory without saying what the building actually is, like a really easy treasure map. I'm going to call it Les Fauves after the group of French artists from he early 20th century."

"Like as in Matisse and Derain, the beasts?" George Henri knew them well.

"It's actually the wild beasts."

"What is it?" Castor asked.

"It was a group of artists in Paris around the early 20th century." George Henri said. "They had a movement called Fauvism that was inspired by a teacher, his name was… Gustave, Gustave Moreau. I remember Matisse saying that he didn't set them on the right road, but off the roads. Some of the most influential impressionist painters came out of the movement."

"And that's what is happening. They had Gustave, and we have Delbert Peach, and they had Montparnasse, Paris, and now we have Williamsburg, Brooklyn." I said.

"I believe in you buddy." Castor said with a slur while he wrapped his arm around my shoulder.

"Castor, I know you're not drunk."

CHAPTER 24

ROD FARTHING

WHEN I woke on that October morning I thought it must have been a Tuesday or Thursday and the Madonna Arm's workout was in full effect, but it wasn't those days. Then I thought it must be Sunday and the Times Up folks were doing their bike workshop, but it wasn't that day either. Then I thought that it must be Saturday when the farmer's market people set up shop downstairs, but it wasn't that day either. I crawled out of bed genuinely confused about time. When I walked out my door someone yelled, "Cut! What the hell! Who opened that door?"

I looked out into the hall at a film crew. "Me. I live here."

"Are you leaving?"

"I was going to take a piss if that's alright with you?"

"Okay, fuck it. Let's take ten minutes. Everybody take a piss and we'll regroup."

I noticed a half naked girl as I was going in the bathroom. That made me a little less angry. When I came out she was walking down the stairs, so I followed her. I was going to ask what they were filming until it became very clear on its own. The guy with the giant dick hanging out of his open robe let me know they were shooting a porn movie.

"Hey guy who lives here, can we go back to making our film?"

"Yeah man, do it." I went outside. Castor was talking to Abe in the street.

"How awesome is this?" Castor had a big grin on his face.

"Are you going to be in it?" I joked, but I should have known better.

"I'm trying. Apparently the girls have all been tested. They said I still have to wear a condom though."

"Unbelievable. They don't trust you of all people!"

"Yeah, I feel kind of offended."

"So are you like a stand-in? Like if one of the guys can't get it up?"

"Yeah I guess so, but the director said they are going to see how it all plays out. If another man makes sense they'll bring me in. I even have a porn name, Rod Farthing."

"Good luck Rod. I'm going to go down to the Domino factory and try to forget any of this ever happened."

I had been going in the factory, cleaning up, and setting up the space. Before all the condos and free-range markets and Duane Reade's, that area on Kent was a desolate row for delivery trucks to speed from the Navy Yards to Green Point. There was no one around to question any suspicious activity.

Later on I went to work because it turned out the day was actually Wednesday. I had been picking up my very own bartending shifts on hump-day. Nicolette and George Henri came to keep me company. I told them about the porn film and of course they thought it was hilarious.

"I don't know how much more I can take." I told them. "Every day it's something else in my face."

"You can move in with me." George Henri said sexually joking.

"I can be your room maid for rent."

"In that case you can move in with me." Nicolette said.

"I'll keep you both in mind. Five hundred a month is going to be hard to beat no matter who I sleep with."

We were just a couple weeks away from the Les Fauves event. Nicolette had just self published a book of poetry and wanted to debut it at the event. George Henri had his new collection ready to unveil to the public. The Secrets were going to have their official cd release show to end the party. I had almost finished my book and was going to read an excerpt from its first draft pages.

I thought that life was finally coming together. It felt easy like walking. At the very least, I thought it was going to let me have a little breathing room.

CHAPTER 25

LES FAUVES EN FEU

THE power went out again. It was happening at least twice a night. Our old building couldn't handle the amount of electricity needed to support the dozen RV's out on South 6th Street. I had been writing by candlelight at the table in our kitchen. That night I was finishing up the piece I was going to read at the Les Fauves event, which was less than 20 hours away at that moment.

After the second power outage of the night, I lost my cool, went out to the RV's, and began screaming at the gypsy hipsters. "You dick-fucks are the worst thing to happen to my existence! I've been putting up with your shit for almost two months and I'm fucking done. I've got a million fucking things to do before tomorrow and I won't be bothered by you again. I'm unplugging this bullshit of a electricity system and I don't want to hear one fucking peep from you for the next ten hours!"

The ringleader Dusty came up to me calmly and said, "Hey man. Sorry about that. We didn't know that we were bothering you. Anything you need just let me and the guys know. We got it. What do you need?"

I inhaled and exhaled for a bit while staring him down, and then asked, "Seriously?"

"For sure man, seriously."

"I'll be right back." They weren't aware of it, but these guys owed me big. I went upstairs, got a list of things that needed to be done by the next day, and gave it to Dusty to take care of. Probably not the best decision, but desperation was kicking in. I went back to my kitchen and lit three more candles. Shadows and light danced over my words. I took a candle to my walls for reference. There must have been a whole book on my bedroom walls by then. Back under the dancing light the story poured out like never before. The release of my duties must have loosened the bricks in my head. I wrote until the early morning and then crashed for a couple of hours. When I woke up I went into a state of panic. The words on the wall were jumbled. My internal clock claimed I slept through the night.

I ran downstairs and found Dusty. "What happened? Did people show up?"

"Show up where?"

"What time is it?"

"I don't know. Like noon probably."

I backed off and tried to grasp reality. The weather had changed. It was crisp, almost cold. Did I sleep through November?

"So we got everything together." Dusty said. "I mean I think we did. I lost the list. I mean I didn't lose it. I gave it to Joe, and Joe gave it to someone else, and they lost it."

I started laughing in relief. "Thank you so much Dusty. I'm sure whatever you did was plenty."

"Rad. Can we turn the power back on now? It's freezing in those campers."

"Yeah, thanks for being nice about all that. I was under a lot of pressure. You're not really the worst thing to happen to my existence."

"I know. I've known people that I've been the worst thing to happen to, and you're nothing like them."

"Well, that's impressive either way. I'm going to head down to the factory."

I biked down to the Domino building. When I walked inside I couldn't believe it. It looked great. The gypsy hipsters finally did something right. There were still a lot of things to do before six o'clock. I rode over to George Henri's to help him with the paintings. He was still sleeping. He finally opened the door after I beat on it for several minutes.

"George Henri. Let's go buddy!"

He went back to bed. "Leave me be young Alex. I had a hell of a night last night. I fell in love at least three times, and out of love four."

"I'll be back in two hours jerk."

"Love you too."

I went back to 99 and thanked the guys for their help.

"No problem." Dusty said. "I'm excited about the poetry reading."

"It's not a poetry reading, but there will be a couple people reading their poems."

"Oh, so what do you call it?"

"It's… a mixed art event I guess."

"But you're reading your poems?"

"No, I write stories, not poems."

"I write poems. Maybe I can read at the mixed art event." He said.

"Yeah, maybe." I couldn't say no. Who knows? His poems might be worth hearing.

"Rad, I'll get a couple together just in case. Is there anything else we can help you with?"

"Yeah, actually I still need someone to pick up beer and ice, and I need the Christmas tree lights put up around the stage area. Can you handle that? Or mind doing it? I mean I can do it, but I'm kind of crunched on time."

"For sure bro, no worries, we got it."

"Thank you so much. The coolers are in the backyard, and the lights are up in the office."

I gave him $200 to get as many cases of PBR that could afford. Then I went to get four handles of whiskey. It was going to be a beer and whiskey bar only, like the cowboy days. When I got back, the coolers were gone so I took that as a good sign. Then I went upstairs and saw that they hadn't taken the lights. I grabbed the lights and whiskey and headed down to the factory to help them out. The Secrets still had to load in their equipment and do a sound check. A pressure was building in my head. Nobody was on time, and I was going to explode.

I walked straight down South 6th to Kent. When I turned on Kent there was a fire truck down near the factory. Two more trucks passed by me with their sirens blaring and lights flashing. Then I saw Dusty and crew running at me from behind the fence at South 5th. They had obviously run around the dockside from the setup point. They climbed the fence and we got out of view of the authorities.

"Bro, the fire department came!"

"I see. What happened?" I thought that they probably just got word of the event and came to shut it down.

"Come on. We should probably get out of here." We rapidly walked up 5th while Dusty explained to me that they thought that it would be too cold to throw the event in the factory. He got the brilliant idea that the space was big enough to hold large, yet contained flames. They gathered enough metal fixtures and beams to make two fire-pits. Then they took all those unused wooden pallets and turned the cold factory space into something out of an apocalyptic movie.

"It was awesome, you should have seen it." Dusty told me. "But then all of a sudden we heard sirens. Joe goes to platform, sees the fire truck coming. That's when we bolted."

I was devastated.

"You would think that they would just let that place burn to the ground." Joe said.

I remembered when I first met Delbert Peach and I told him how I pictured the Domino factory on fire when it processed in my mind. Now, there I was running away from the premonition.

Dusty kept rambling on about what they should have done, but I couldn't hear him. All that work for nothing, is what I heard. I went to my bedroom and put my face into a pillow. A sharp pain was shooting through my head. I didn't know what to do. I guess I figured I would just go down and put a sign on the fence that says the event is cancelled. Cancel the night, cancel the year, cancel life.

Then there was a knock on my door.

"What?"

"It's Abe. Can I come in?"

I opened the door to that intense indifferent stare of Abe. "So Dusty burned down your party?"

"Seems so."

"He's not dependable. He's undependable."

"Thank you Abe. I figured that out."

"But he does mean well."

"Thank you Abe. I just want to be by myself."

"Well, I came with an offer if you'd like to hear it?"

I briefly ran through a list ideas that Abe would throw at me. They mostly had to do with farm animals and underage girls.

"I think we should have it here instead."

"Here at 99? The downstairs?"

"Yeah, I'll get in touch with all my people and tell them it's here. All the guys outside said they'd help get it together. They do mean well you know?"

"Abe, I think this might be your best idea ever. I'll go down to the factory after the fire department leaves and put a sign telling people to come to 99. I don't know how we're going fit everyone, but it's better than letting it go I suppose."

I went downstairs and delegated duties to all of the RV crew. "First of all. No fires!"

"Do you still want the beer and ice?" Dusty had the money in his hand.

"I thought you left it in the factory?"

"Nah, we just took the coolers down and then got distracted by the idea about the fire-pits."

"Your distractions have seemed to work out in some way." I said. "Get the beer and find one big cooler. We'll put the rest in our refrigerator."

In less than three hours we transformed 99 into the music venue art space that it once was in the 80's. George Henri was able to display about twenty of his pieces. The band minimalized their playing space to where they were almost on top of each other. The storage room in the back was cleared out to be the bar.

We started an hour late. By the time that night had fallen, the downstairs was filled and there were another hundred or so bodies out by South 6th Street shantytown. There were people there that I wouldn't have ever expected, including the nice guy with the Socials that we kicked out of Pete's Candy Store, including Paige who's claim to fame was that she "hated art," including Foxcroft's sister Arien who I hadn't seen since we took each other away for a second, and even the screaming Haitian that respectfully didn't scream that night. Abe had done a stand-up job. There were hipsters, Williamsburg Puerto Ricans, Hasid's, Manhattan Socials, literary academia's, Bushwick art curators, and all others in between that all shared the commonality of having ears.

Then there were the four friends that met on that rooftop on New Years Eve almost a year before.

We all shared a feeling of hunger, empty bellies, bottomless appetites that when filled kept us up at night. When we spoke we shouted, all our voices together, a chorus of pleas and protests, rooftop dreams, voices carrying from building to building, no sky scrapers to block them, we all shared a voice, devouring the ears that accepted it, that opened to us. We would be heard. We would dizzily take in those sunrise nights and talk about what it would be like to be heard.

Later on after the crowd had wound down and we had time to breathe and drink, Dusty came up to me. He offered me a cigarette and said, "It was kind of like a… what do they call it? A blessing in disguise."

"Yeah." I laughed. "We'll just call it that."

"I'm serious. If the fire department would have came for just a couple little fires, they would have come or the police definitely would have come to the factory for this party, I mean… mixed art event."

He may have been right. It's hard to say how all the desperate faults in the universe sometimes work toward what we truly need. All I know is that night worked out perfectly. After I gave Abe his cut of the bar, he exclaimed that it was a success. Delbert told me once that, 'Success equals how comfortably one can progress towards death.' I have to admit that after the Les Fauves I was feeling pretty damn comfortable. It gave us that voice, that chance to prove to ourselves that what we were doing wasn't useless. That night we could breathe a little easier.

Chapter 26

500 JAPANESE BICYCLES

WHEN the bikes came, the dream was almost over. 500 Japanese bicycles shipped in one crate to 99 South 6th Street.

"What are you going to do with these?" I asked Abe as they unloaded the cargo. Most of the bikes were trash. They were in pieces, broken and rusted, and on top of all that they required special tools that no one on this side of the Earth had.

"Fix them, and sell them. Every hipster in Brooklyn will want one." Abe said.

"No, I meant right now. What are you going to do with them right now?"

"Yes, that was something that hadn't quite been thought out. I think were going to get a really long cable and tie them all together down the sidewalk."

But that didn't happen. They were able to tie about half of them, which left another 250 bikes that were put downstairs, in the backyard, in Abe's office, and to my ultimate dismay, they filled up the balcony with the old frames and tires. Abe bartered the telescope away for another RV. That's when I wasn't sure anymore about 99, about Abe's agenda that I thought was a subconscious agenda toward beauty. I wasn't so sure anymore after the telescope was taken away. Abe and 99 had given me enough beauty for a lifetime. There was the death of Foxcroft, there was no heat, there was no hot water, there were strangers in my bathroom daily, there were squatters downstairs, there was waking up at all hours of the night to show people the stars, there was the shantytown, there was the power outages, there was the Madonna Arms, there was the bicycle workshops, and there was still the anxiety that Abe would follow up on his underage/all hours bar.

99 had created a year of magic, but that time was almost over. That night of Les Fauves was the end of the beginning. It's now been years since that magical night, but it carries on.

If you mention Les Fauves to anyone in the Williamsburg area they almost always know that it was the time when the poem *Rooftop Dreams* was read, it was the first time the song *The Bedford Kids* was played live, it was the first time anyone saw the *Black Eye* collection, and it was the first time anyone had heard about the story of the hipster chickens. It was a night of influence, of inspiration for the destined ones to strive to be heard.

At some point when I was reading at the event, I looked up into the crowd. In the back was a man in a hoodie and sunglasses. I'm pretty sure it was Delbert Peach. When I was done I tried to get to the back where he was, but it was so packed, that by the time I got there he had disappeared once again. I went all around inside and out looking for him, but I guess just like before, he had come for a brief moment in time to see us off into our new lives.

Our destinies were all sparked in that year of 2006. We were lucky to have each other. It was needed to make whatever web of artistic energy possible. Any loose ends and it would have never formed. And then like almost all New York relationships, we naturally went our separate ways.

Nicolette won a bilingual poetry award and was offered a yearlong fellowship in Belgium. Castor Hazel and The Secrets ended up releasing three successful LP's before breaking up years later. George Henri had several art dealers fighting over his collection. He decided to display in the 99 Gallery in Chelsea, based solely on superstition of the number. Every piece eventually sold. He overdosed two years later and the *Black Eye* collection turned from obscure paintings to personal treasures. As far as anyone knew they were the only paintings he completed after the fire.

And then there was me...

Chapter 27

PORTABLE SECOND

I was working in the Ale House the night before I was to leave for the holidays. It would be the first time I visited my family in almost two years. At around three in the morning, like the equivalent to midnight in the fairytales, she walked in. Our eyes locked and we said nothing. She once again sat at the end of the bar by that bookshelf. I took her a glass of wine as her small hand reached up to grab a large book titled, *To Be Heard: The Complete Collection of the Misfit Poets of the 20th Century.*

I had never read any of those books on the shelf. I had never stopped thinking about her, and those last words we parted with. "You're going to finish what you need to finish and then you'll start something new. I'm going to be what's new."

I had almost just finished what I needed to finish. My walls were full. My notebooks were full. I just needed to finish my book before I went back to my hometown. This was something important to all of us, a feeling of accomplishment, a feeling of worth. We needed some sort of validation, some proof that we were doing it, and it was all for ourselves, because everyone else that loved us, loved us for who we were, not for our haunted dreams and for our need to be validated. We pushed forward into the dreadful holidays, but this time we all went back to our former homes and former friends and family with our heads held high, ready to face that new year.

When she took that book down off the shelf and broke her stare from my eyes, I followed her eyes to the cover of the book. I laughed to myself, and took out my notebook. "Your timing is unbelievable." I wrote down in the last page of my notebook: TITLE OF NOVEL: TO BE HEARD. Then it was finished.

"Isn't it always." She said. "God almost always knows what it's doing."

I studied her to figure out if she was serious or not, because I truly believed in the mystical immanent presence of a God. Then she smiled, and I was even more unsure. But that's what *she* does. I would come to find this out on a daily basis. What would I never do? At the end of the year I moved out of 99 and in with her. She was the new thing. She would smile and I would always be unsure.

And that was it I suppose, the end of 2006 in Williamsburg. I suppose that's as good as any place to stop. Delbert used to tell me that everything was valid, and as right as he always was, this moment, after what seemed like the victory after a bloody battle, it seemed that moment was a second more valid than all the other valid moments. Just as one can't ever get back to Montparnasse, Paris to capture those days with the Lost Generation, just as one can't ever get back to North Beach, San Francisco to those days with the Beat Generation, one can't get back to those days in Williamsburg, Brooklyn with my generation. But the ghosts will always be there, the ghosts will haunt, the ghosts will inspire, the ghosts will stay young and hungry, and they will be there to remind us of a time period.

Incidentally there was an extra second added on to the world clock that year right before going into 2007. I liked to think that they did it for us, as if they knew that was *our* second in the universe. Delbert once told me that all of mankind could be summed up in one second's time. It was all just a flash and the only reason for denominations of time was to comprehend that we had a chance to live.

Thank *God* we got that chance!

THE END